GONE COUNTRY

KATRINA MARIE

Gone Country © 2019 by Dreamer Books LLC. All rights reserved.

No part of this book may be reproduced in any form or by any electronic or mechanical means, including photography, recording, or by information storage and retrieval system, without written permission of the author, except where permitted by law.

This book is a work of fiction. Names, places, characters, and incidents are the product of author's imagination or are used fictitiously.

Editor: VMC Art & Design & Small Edits

Cover design © A Novel Idea Services

Mom and Dad
Thank you for always believing in me.

Chapter One

ALMOST JUMPING OUT MY SEAT, the shrill ring of my phone scares the hell out of me as I knock over my coffee right onto my keyboard. *Son of a bitch. I swear this shit only happens to me.* The IT department is not going to be happy with me in the morning.

My phone stops ringing for a whole two seconds before it starts again. I answer it without looking at the screen, "Hello?"

"Stella," Tiffany, my cousin, yells. "Come to the club with us tonight. It'll be fun." She sing-songs the last part because she knows it gets on my nerves.

"Sorry. I can't tonight. I need to get this report done for my boss."

"Don't tell me you're still at the office," Tiffany scolds. "I swear all you do is work. It's okay to take a break, you do know that, right?"

It's the same fight, over and over again. Both of my cousins think I work too much. But they don't understand. If I don't outperform everyone else, I won't get the promotion I've had my eye on for months.

"Yes," I huff, throwing paper towels over the liquid, hoping it will soak up because if not my keyboard's a goner. "I know that I can take a break, but he needs these reports first thing Monday morning."

"But it's Saturday," my cousin whines. "You should be out enjoying life, not holed up in your cubicle. You're only twenty-nine, come on *live a little*."

"Tiff. I have a life. It may not be yours, but I have one." I scoop all the drenched paper towels into the trash can. "I'll be up and ready for brunch in the morning. You and Audrey will manage just fine without me tonight."

"I guess," she mutters, her voice no longer holding the excitement it had only moments ago. "We'll see you in the morning." She hangs up without telling me bye.

It's then that I know I've hurt her feelings. She always ends our calls with "bye, I love you." It started when we were kids and missing each other minutes after leaving the other's house. Audrey does it, too, just not as much. Audrey is the logical one of us, always thinking problems through. Tiffany, though…she's the free spirit and goes wherever the wind takes her.

We've always been thick as thieves. Summers at each other's houses, and always on the phone any chance we got. We knew at a very early age that we would always be more than cousins, we'd be best friends.

Hell, they moved to the same city I live in so we could be around each other. Others might see it as weird, but these two are my best friends. They are the ones who get me when most people don't. Well, that was true until I started this job. Now they say I work too hard and don't give myself any time off. If I didn't love what I do and have my eyes set on that coveted promotion, I could see where it might be a problem. However, I'm going after my goals and dream job. I only wish they could be more understanding. I think Audrey might, but not enough to keep from siding with Tiffany every time she brings it up.

There's no use dwelling on it. I need to finish up these reports, but I press the enter key on my sticky keyboard nothing happens. *Damn it, this is not good.* There's no way I'll finish compiling these if I can't get this to work. I write a quick note to the tech department to let them know about my keyboard. I'll have to drop it by there on my way out of the building and hope I don't trip over any of the five thousand wires they have everywhere. Seriously, they could clean it up some.

It looks like I'll be getting out of here early after all. But I'm not going to be clubbing with my cousins. I can access my work files from my laptop at home, thank God. Otherwise, I'd fail in my task. I can't let that happen.

Gathering my things and some paper from the printer, I make my way out of the office.

As I walk through my apartment door, the only thing that greets me is silence. I will admit that it's a little sad, but with all the hours I put in at the office, having a pet doesn't make sense. It wouldn't be fair for them to be cooped up in the house all day, and only getting my attention when I squeeze a bit of time away from my work duties.

Throwing my bag on the sofa, I glance at the end table. The normally green aloe vera plant is turning brown at the tips. *When did I last water this thing?* It's the only plant I've managed to keep alive. I've never claimed to have a green thumb, but I'm trying. If anything, my cousins will be happy to have a fresh supply of aloe to soothe their sunburns this summer.

Speaking of, I pull my phone out of my pocket, hoping to have a text from Tiffany. No such luck. She must still be angry with me. I don't blame her, not really. Yet, she knows how important this promotion is to me. I've been talking about it for months. I am always there to support her when she goes after everything she wants even when she gets burned from following ridiculous dreams. Right now, the only person I'm getting encouragement from is Audrey, and even she is giving me the cold shoulder. They'll get over it, though. Or, I hope they will. I can't imagine them being pissed at me for longer than a day.

My laptop sits on my coffee table, and I press the power button. While it's booting up, I tap on the Instagram app from my phone. I don't even have to scroll to find a picture of the girls at the bar. It's the first picture that pops up. I can barely see Audrey and Tiffany in the dark club, but the neon lights are illuminating their faces just enough for me to make out some of their features. Any other night, and I'd be in the picture with them. Instead, I'm at home, working.

A pang of jealousy rips through me, and I squash it down. I chose this. I could be out, dancing until my feet hurt, but this job is more important right now. This promotion is important. Once I get it, I'll be able to give myself a little more downtime. The need to bust my ass in order to prove my worth will not be a burden I have to bear for much longer. At least, that's what I keep telling myself, anyway. I double tap the image, and I hope they know I'm with them in spirit.

This stupid computer is still loading, so I change into a pair of sweatpants and a t-shirt. If I have to work, I'm going to be comfortable while doing it. It would be great if they'd allow me to work from home sometimes. I mean, I already do so much here that I never even get recognized, or compensated for. But, that's okay, once I finally get that promotion, I'll have a bit more freedom and can pass some minor things off to someone else. Though, that's not likely to happen too often. It's the same thing that's being done to me now, and it can be frustrating. Half the shit I do isn't even under my job description, but I keep doing it because I don't want to piss off my direct boss, Mr. Granger.

Settling on the sofa, I pull the laptop onto my legs and prop my feet on the coffee table. Having to redo everything that I've already done is going to suck, but I don't want them to have a reason to overlook me when they start announcing promotion candidates. That would be a punch in the gut after all the work, and time, I've put in.

The silence is overwhelming, so I turn on my TV for background noise. At the office silence is never an issue. There's always some sort of noise, whether it be someone walking past my desk, talking on the phone, or the whirring of the computers and copiers. Flipping through the channels, I settle on reruns of *Charmed* and turn the volume just loud enough to mask the stillness of my apartment. It's going to be a struggle not to watch.

Hours later my vision is blurring from shuffling between spreadsheets, and I desperately want to call it a night. The only thing pushing me forward is the desire to be offered what I want so much. I can see my dream job dangling on a string in front of me. There is nothing more important to me, except maybe my cousins, than earning that spot in the company.

Chapter Two

SOMETHING SLAMS INTO ME, and my eyes pop open. *What the actual fuck?*

Tiffany's face, framed by her long red hair, fills my view. "Good morning, Sunshine," she smirks.

"I'm really regretting giving you a key to my apartment," I groan. "Move so I can sit up."

Tiffany snorts, "I lost my copy months ago."

"What?" I shriek. She's just now telling me this?

She shrugs, and moves away from me. "We used Audrey's key to get in. She has it hidden in her purse to make sure she doesn't lose it."

I glare at her. "Maybe you should take a note from her book, and do the same."

I must have fallen asleep while working last night. Sitting up, I frantically search for my laptop. If that thing is broken from falling off my lap, I might as well quit my job and look for another one. "I moved it to the table," Audrey announces from the other side of the room. Thank God she had the good sense to move it before our youngest cousin attacked me.

Gone Country

"Thank you," I sigh. I'd lose it if something else happened to those reports. "Why are y'all here?" Glancing at the clock on the wall, the hands are at eight. It's way too early to be dealing with my cousins. "Brunch isn't for another few hours."

"Would you believe me if I said it's because we really missed you?" Tiffany fluttered her eyelashes. She's not fooling anyone with the sweet and innocent act.

"Nope," I shake my head. "Last night you were pissed at me for not going out. You are a grudge holder, and I know better. Why are you really here?"

"Whatever," she rolls her eyes and stomps toward the kitchen. My downstairs neighbors are not going to be happy about that.

Audrey walks across the room and sits on the sofa beside me, way too close for comfort. "She wanted to make sure you actually showed up for brunch, and this is the only way she could think of to do it."

I scoff. These two are too much, and are being absolutely ridiculous. "I have never missed our weekly brunch. And honestly, I'm a little hurt that y'all think so little of me." Audrey and Tiffany may be family, but they are also my best friends.

"Can you blame us?" Tiffany comes back into the living room with cups, orange juice, and the only bottle of vodka I have. "You have never turned down an offer to go out for a night on the town in the past. Hell, we've barely heard from you for the past few weeks. You are always shut away in your tiny office at work." She takes a second to nod toward my laptop. "You're even bringing work home."

I've tried to explain how important this position is to Tiffany but she doesn't get it. "The only reason I brought work home last night is because I spilled coffee all over my keyboard at the office when I answered your call." The sad thing is, I still have work to do since I fell asleep in the middle of it last night.

Audrey grabs the cups from Tiffany and sets them on the coffee table. "Why did you phrase it like that?" She eyes me while Tiffany fills the cups with orange juice. "How often are you bringing work home?"

Damn it. She would be the one to pick apart my sentences. I don't want to admit how often I bring stuff home. They would never stop giving me shit for it.

"From the silence," Tiffany says while adding more vodka than necessary to the cups. "She brings shit home a lot more often than she'd have us think." She picks up one of the cups and hands it to me. "Am I right?"

"Ugh," I groan. "Fine, you're right. Is that what you want to hear? I've been bringing a lot of work home." Tiffany opens her mouth to add her two cents, but I cut her off. I can't let more of her negativity fill the air. "I can't keep up with everything they are giving me, but I want to prove that I can handle anything, and that I'm ready for more responsibilities and deserve the promotion."

"Are they paying you for the hours you are working here?" Audrey purses her lips.

"Well," I draw the word out, stalling. "They don't know I've been doing it."

"That's the dumbest shit I've ever heard," Tiffany yells. "If you are busting your ass during your downtime, you should be compensated for it." She stands up and paces back and forth in front of my TV. "You work way to fucking much, Stella." She whirls around to face me, pointing her finger at me. "You can't enjoy life if you are cooped up in a building all day. How the hell are you going to meet someone, or fall in love? I mean, it's already affecting how much time you spend with us, your best friends." She stomps her foot. "No guy is going to put up with that, or want to come second to your job." She plops down on the floor. Her tantrum obviously over.

"Who said I was looking for a relationship?" I argue. "I'm focusing on me and getting my career underway. Men are the absolute last thing on my mind."

"Tiff has a point," Audrey says, barely above a whisper. "When is the last time you went on a date?"

"Does it matter?" I sigh. "When did this become the interrogate Stella show?"

"We only want to make sure you are doing what's best for you." Audrey grabs my hand and squeezes it. "We don't want you to lose yourself to this job and end up with regret."

"Fine," I relent. "I'll do my best to stop taking on more than I can handle." At least as far as they know. Nothing will stop me from achieving my goals. Pulling my hand from Audrey's, I stand up. "Now, let me get ready. I'm going to need food soon with the amount of vodka Tiffany put in those drinks."

After the strong drinks Tiffany poured us this morning, we Uber to brunch. There's no reason any of us need to drive. Traffic is busy for a Sunday morning and honking horns aren't helping the lingering bad moods. Most of the negative vibes are coming straight from Tiffany, still bitter about last night.

The driver pulls up to Trudy's, and puts the car in park. We step out into the warm and humid air. I really wish Fall or Winter would make their return. I'm over all this heat. One day I'll visit a place that experiences all four seasons, instead of this Texas heat. My cousins are ahead of me and walk into the restaurant without looking back to see if I am with them. I'm so caught up in my head, that I don't notice the door closing, and walk straight into it. When am I going to learn that I'm almost incapable of doing two things at once? However, it doesn't escape my notice that Tiffany didn't hold the door open for me. I hope karma is a real bitch, and they are out of her favorite drink.

"Thanks a lot, cuz," I smack her arm when I catch up to them.

"Oh, I'm sorry," she pitches her voice high. "I thought you were right behind me." She smirks before walking toward the hostess stand. She's such a liar. Her being mad is understandable, but she doesn't have to be a bitch about it.

The restaurant is packed, more than usual, and even though we are regulars, we have to wait for a table to open up. It's probably because we're here earlier than usual thanks to Tiffany and Audrey showing up at my apartment at the ass crack of dawn. This is one of the only places I'll actually wait for a table to open up. The food is that good. The drinks are too, and I weave around other patrons until I'm standing in front of the bar. I need more alcohol to deal with the animosity I'm feeling around my cousins. We've fought plenty of times, but this time feels different. As if it's hit Tiffany harder than usual. She has to be going through something she's not telling us about. The difference is, I won't pester her until she wants to beat me.

Since I'm a good cousin, and don't act like an ass when I'm frustrated, I save the first three seats that become available before ordering my drink. We are going to be here for a bit before our table is called, might as well get comfortable. I text both girls since they went to the restroom while I searched out seats for us.

Stella: Come to the bar. I've got us some seats until our table is ready.
Audrey: On our way
Tiffany: Did you also get us drinks? I'm thirsty.

Leave it to her to only think about herself. No thanks, or anything. Just a question in return. I don't respond to their texts. They will see as soon as they get over here. No matter how much they drive me crazy, I'm mature enough to make sure they are taken care of. I mean, I'm not a completely horrible person.

I'm eavesdropping on the conversation happening next to me when Audrey and Tiffany take their seats. The man and woman are arguing about not getting enough of the other's attention. That, right there, is one of the main reasons I'm glad to be single. There's no way in hell I'd be able to juggle both my job and a needy relationship.

Coming up behind me, I hear Tiffany's voice, "You are seriously the best," she reaches for her drink and wraps her lips around the straw of her Bloody Mary. I guess all is forgotten, at least for now. "Thank you, Stella." She puts her hand over mine and gives me a rueful smile. Finally, she's done being bitchy. I hate fighting with my two favorite people. It makes things weird, and while usually we're a handful when we're together…we can be assholes when we're fighting. Nobody likes being around us during those times.

"You're welcome," I answer. "A little pre-food drinking

is better than waiting around, doing nothing. And it's the perfect pairing for chips and salsa."

They nod in agreement, grabbing a chip and dipping it in the salsa at the same time. If you didn't know better, you'd think they are sisters. Hell, everyone already does since they have names revolving around Audrey Hepburn. That's not the case though. Their moms are really close to each other and have had their names picked out since they thought about having children. They were obsessed with watching old Hepburn movies, and one chose Audrey while the other chose Tiffany after their favorite movie. Since Mom married into the family, she definitely wasn't prepared to follow the crowd on naming me after a Hepburn character. My aunts weren't thrilled about it, but they've become closer throughout the years. "How's everything going with y'all this week? With all the hours I'm working, I'm out of the loop. Give me all the details."

Tiffany rolls her eyes at me. "You'd know that if you weren't at work all the time."

"Can we not go through this again?" The glass in my hand thuds against the bar top a little harsher than intended. It's just that I'm sick of going back to this every single time she opens her mouth. "We're here to have brunch and hang out. Not go over every single thing I'm doing that pisses you off."

"Fine," she shrugs. "Things have been going well. A new guy moved into the building over the week."

"He must be a looker if you've noticed him." As the free-spirit of the group, Tiffany goes wherever the wind blows her. She doesn't stick with relationships long and usually flutters off to the next guy whenever things start getting serious. I have to give her props, at least she's putting herself out there. She'll never be like me and practically married to her job.

"He's not really my type," she sighs. Yep, she's interested.

"I didn't realize you had a type," Audrey snorts.

"Shut up, asshole," she bumps our cousin's shoulder. "At least, I have the guts to talk to men. You sit over there all shy, and meek, expecting me to do all the work for you."

"I can't help it if I get nervous. Stupid shit comes out of my mouth every time I've attempted to approach someone." Audrey takes a sip of her drink and shrugs. "I can't help that I'm awkward."

I need to steer this conversation in another direction or else they are going to start fighting. "How's work going Audrey?"

"Same old, same old." She's been working at the same company for years, and nothing ever changes one way or the other. "Another year without a raise, but it's okay since nobody else is getting one either."

"Girl, I don't see how you are still working there." Breaking a chip in half, I dip it in the salsa. "You get more responsibilities added on, but don't get anything else in return."

"It's easy," she says. "I know what I'm doing, and I don't have to try too hard."

That is the lamest excuse I've ever heard. It fits her, though. She's always been the content one. I always want more, and Tiffany only wants to be able to do whatever she desires. We are completely different, and yet, somehow, we manage to click so well.

I'm dying to give her my opinion on the whole job thing when the buzzer on the bar for our table vibrates.

Suddenly, my thoughts shift to what I'm going to order. I'm thinking enchiladas sound amazing right now. Weaving through the crowd toward the hostess stand isn't any easier. If anything, I think more people are here than before. After a quick glance at my phone, I sigh. We've already been here for almost an hour. If we decide to go shopping afterward, as is customary, I'm going to run out of time to get these reports finished.

Halfway through our meal, I jump when my cell phone vibrates against the table. The only people that would call me, besides my parents, are sitting directly in front of me. When the girls see who is calling, they groan in unison.

"Go ahead and answer it," Tiffany waves toward the phone. "I know your fingers are itching to hit the accept call button." She makes it sound like I'm having some secret affair.

My fingers creep toward the phone. The only thing keeping me from picking it up and answering is the scowl on Tiffany's face. If I answer, I'm drawing a line in the sand showing my cousins that I value my job more than I value my time with them. That's not the case, though. Instead of hurting their feelings, I press the button to mute it and let it go to voicemail. I can't believe I just did that. While this is a smart move in my relationship with Audrey and Tiffany, it could very well bite me in the ass at work. I have never ignored a call from my boss, even when I was down with the flu. Only time will tell what this disregard will cost me in the long run.

Tiffany's eyes widen, no doubt surprised by my behavior. It's definitely not normal, at least not for me. She doesn't acknowledge it any more than that and continues telling her story about her latest dating adventure. I swear, if this girl continues to go out with whoever direct messages her on all of those dating apps, she's going to wind up missing one day. She has exactly zero screening process when she agrees to go out with these men. It's a good thing her mama is none the wiser. She would throw a fit if she knew, and I won't be the one to fill her in any time soon.

My phone begins vibrating again, and it's Audrey that sighs this time. "You might as well answer it. Your boss isn't going to let up until you do."

She's right, even though I wish she wasn't. "Okay. Let me just see what he wants." I grab the phone and my finger hovers above the screen. "Maybe it's nothing and we can forget he ever called."

Swiping across the screen, I accept the call. "Hello?" Please be something I can answer now and not require me to put my cousins on the back burner once again.

"Stella, thank God you answered." My boss sounds frazzled, and that is never a good sign. At least, not for me. I swear this man can't do anything without me. It should be complementary, but hell, I'd love to be able to go a day without him acting as if everything is falling apart around him.

"Is everything okay?" I regret asking as soon as the words leave my mouth. Of course, something is wrong. He wouldn't be calling me otherwise.

"Have you finished those reports?" No, but I'm not going to tell him that. "I didn't see them in my email, and I need to go over them for tomorrow's meeting."

Of course, that's why he's blowing up my phone. I usually have the reports sent to him before I leave the office on Friday. The only bad thing is, they still aren't done, and I have absolutely nothing to send him. "I'm so sorry, sir. It must have slipped my mind." It didn't.

Another thing he doesn't need to know.

"Can you get them sent to me today?" *Damn it*. His voice is strained and irritated. Not that I blame him. This is completely out of the norm for me. "I really need them tonight."

"N-no problem," I stutter. I hate letting people down. Especially, those that can affect my income. "I'm actually not home right now, but as soon as I get home, I will email them over."

"Thank you, Stella." His voice is cold, and I know I've disappointed him. The call is ended before I can utter another word.

"I'm guessing it wasn't a good call?" Audrey takes a bite of her enchiladas. Gee, I wonder how she guessed.

"Not even a little bit," I reply. "I'm going to have to skip out on shopping today, girls. Apparently, my boss needs this report right now, and after we're done eating, I'm going home to make sure I don't lose my job."

Tiffany mutters something under her breath, but I don't catch it. I'm not sure I want to know because it can't be good. And so begins round three of being pissed at Stella. It's frustrating, but some things are more important that shopping with the girls. Sometimes, it sucks being the oldest cousin in our little trio.

Chapter Three

THERE'S a shiny new keyboard sitting in front of my computer when I walk into my tiny office on Monday. Tiffany was wrong when she said I'm just another person in a cubicle. I've worked my ass off to get this small space of my own. I won't be satisfied until I have one of the big offices facing the city skyline. When I adjust my keyboard to precisely where I want it, I see there's a post it note hidden underneath with an annoyed message. *Try not to spill coffee all over this one. Keep it away from the keyboard.*

I swear the folks down in IT don't have any sort of empathy. It's not like I do it on purpose. Bad shit just happens to follow me wherever I go. It's a wonder I haven't broken something just walking and going about my day.

Searching around the room, I look for a wood surface to knock on. I don't need that vibe following me around for the rest of the day. The imitation wood my computer sits on will have to do. I give it three solid taps, and set my coffee down as far away from the keyboard as possible. The note could have been written slightly more tactfully, but I get it. They are replacing things in my office more often than not.

My boss, Mr. Granger, passes by my open door and nods. He's not overly talkative on a normal day, but today he didn't even say good morning. I guess he's still pissed about the reports being late. I knew there would be repercussions for not having them to him as early as I usually do.

A text message comes through on my phone.

Audrey: How much shit are you in with your boss?
Stella: Don't know yet. He just passed by my office and only nodded at me.
Audrey: Well, you can always crash at my house if you get fired and lose your apartment.

Her level of confidence in my situation is worrisome. It's my first somewhat major screw up, there's no way in hell they would fire me for that. Would they?

There's a soft knock on my office door. It opens slowly, and Ellen, the receptionist for our department, pokes her head inside. "Stella, Mr. Hart wants to see you in his office as soon as possible." She closes the door before I have a chance to respond, and scurries away to her desk. *Shit. I am going to be canned*. The big boss never calls anyone into his office without it being bad news. Granger just had to tell the owner about my screw up, and now I'm going to pay for my mistake. Next time, if there is a next time, I'm not leaving the building until everything is finished.

This is one of the things I loathe about working at this company. I have busted my ass to get this far, but I'm expected to drop everything to meet the demands of others. If I wasn't scared, I'd be fired, I wouldn't even bother going to see what Mr. Hart wants. Alas, here I am pushing my chair back and running off the moment he summons me. How am I supposed to do my job if I'm not at my desk?

My heels click clack against the hard floor, earning me curious glances from the customer service employees in the main area. There are usually only two reasons a person is called into the owner's office…you are either being promoted or let go. Worry gnaws at my gut at the prospect of being fired. I just got a bigger apartment and car after spending years saving, and I can't afford to no longer have a job.

Mr. Hart's personal secretary is seated at her desk in front of his office. "Hi Rosie, how are you doing today?"

"Oh, just fine." Her slightly wrinkled hand picks up the cup of coffee sitting in front of her and she takes a sip. She's much older than she looks. It must be all the beauty products she's had delivered here over the years have helped stop the aging process. I only hope to look as great as she does when I'm her age. That's a life goal, right there.

"That's great," I smile. "Um, Mr. Hart asked to speak with me?" Nerves are the only thing I can blame for making that statement come out as a question. Now is not the time for them to shake me up.

Rosie waves toward the door, "Go on in, Dear. He's waiting for you."

"Thanks Rosie," I give her desk a quick tap. Swallowing down my nerves, I knock on Mr. Hart's door twice even though it's open, and step inside. It's time to face whatever is awaiting me inside.

"Oh, Stella, you're here." Mr. Hart is looking at me through his thick wire-rimmed glasses. Honestly, glasses like that should have a plastic frame, but I'm not going to be the one to tell him that. "Come on in and have a seat." He doesn't seem mad, maybe I'm in the clear.

I hurry over to the chair closest to his desk. To most people the seat they choose to sit in wouldn't be a big deal, except it is to me. The chair closest to him shows that I'm not afraid of him, even though I'm terrified of what he could potentially say. "You asked to see me?"

He sets the pen and the paper pad he was writing on aside and meets my gaze. "Yes, I have an opportunity I would like to discuss with you."

A sigh of relief escapes my body without my permission, and I wish I could take it back. It shows a sign of weakness. "What did you have in mind, Sir?"

"We are opening up a new distribution center in Asheville. It's a small town outside the Dallas area." He leans closer as if readying himself to tell me a secret. "I want you to relocate there until the job is complete, and it's running smoothly."

The excitement I had at the word *opportunity* dies with the word *relocation*. I love living in Austin, and moving to a small town, even for a short amount of time, is not in my plan. "Are you sure I'm a right fit for this job? Shouldn't Mr. Granger be doing this since he's the head of operations?" Probably not the best question to follow up with, but I really don't want to move to a small town. I spent my entire life trying to get out of one. Also, Granger will most likely be pissed that I was asked and not him.

He must see that I'm not bouncing with joy to go. "Yes, you are. You aren't afraid to make the hard decisions and get things done. And I think this will be a great opportunity for you to show me that you're ready to lead your own team. You won't be stuck running production reports for people above you, or running errands for them. This will be your baby from the ground up. Making sure the building is ready to go, finding employees to fill it, and training them." He leans back in his chair, waiting for me to say something, and almost falls backwards. Correcting himself and placing his hand over his protruding stomach, he adds, "Did I mention we are also going to pay for the house you'll be staying in, and it comes with a healthy bonus?"

If it means more money in my bank account, and a possible promotion, then I'm one hundred percent in. I could finally give up apartment living and buy a house, maybe find a pet to greet me when I come home. My dislike of small towns is a small thing compared to a better lifestyle for myself. "How healthy are we talking?"

Chapter Four

HOLY SHIT. I walk dazed to my office. That was not at all what I was expecting. Getting called to the boss's office is akin to getting called to the principal's office in grade school. I really don't want to relocate. I'm not even sure how I'd survive without my cousins. They may not support the amount of hours I put into my job, but they have always been there when I need them.

It's a good thing Mr. Hart gave me a few days to think it over. I need Audrey and Tiffany's input. I have a feeling Tiffany will not be happy about the job opportunity. She'll get over it, though. And she can always come visit me. Hell, I'm going to need their help moving all of my crap if I accept the offer.

Stella: I've got big news!!!!
Tiffany: You quit your over-demanding job and found a new one.
Audrey: Are you going to tell us?
Stella: No, Tiff. Yes, Audrey. Want to come over for dinner?

Audrey: See you there!
Tiffany: You're acting like she's going to make it home by dinner.

I swear Tiffany acts like a bitch because she knows it stings a little. Just because she flits from job to job, doing whatever she pleases, doesn't mean I can do the same thing. Her last text doesn't even deserve a response. This is a big deal. At least, it is to me, and I hope both of my cousins support it. I am sort of excited about this opportunity. Well, let's face it, it is really about the bonus, but still.

I look up to see that Mr. Granger is standing in my office door, lips pressed into a firm line. The high of being offered a possible promotion quickly dies. "Stella, can I speak with you?"

Why can't I catch a damn break? I knew he wouldn't be happy that Mr. Hart went around him to talk to me, but I didn't think he'd confront me about it. At least not quite so soon.

"Absolutely, Mr. Granger. What can I do for you?" My smile is plastic and fake. God, I hope I don't resemble some creepy clown.

He walks toward my desk and takes a seat in the only available chair in my office…mine. No excuse me or do you mind. A part of me wants to kick him out of it. The other part knows better than to push my luck. "I understand Mr. Hart gave you a big opportunity."

"Yes, sir," I lean against the window. Damn him for taking my chair. My coffee is inches from him, and I hope he swivels. His dress shirt would be stained brown, and I'd have to keep my laughter inside.

Alas, he doesn't turn. "You cannot screw this up. If you

somehow fail in getting the center up and running, it's not only your job on the line."

Funny, Mr. Hart didn't give me that impression at all. "I'm not a hundred percent sure I'm going to take the offer. He gave me a few days to think it over."

A sly grin crosses Mr. Granger's lips. He obviously has no faith in my capabilities, and that only makes me want to march straight to Mr. Hart's office and accept his offer without a second thought. "You'd be crazy not to take him up on it. I wouldn't wait too long." Without another word, he stands up and walks out.

I love my job; I do, but dealing with asshole bosses is not something I enjoy. Why can't this man help his assistant move up in the company? There's no need for jealousy, or whatever crawled up his ass and died. His reaction to the news only makes me lean toward accepting the offer more than I was earlier. If only to prove him wrong.

I am running late. Tiffany is either going to be very pissed off, or happy because she gets to give me a big fat, I told you so. This time, it's not even because of work. It's all this stupid traffic blocking every direction that leads to my apartment.

For the first time in I don't know how long, I actually left work on time. Not only because I didn't want to hear crap from Tiffany, but also because I'm really excited to tell my cousins about this opportunity. I should have told them to meet me at my apartment later than six. Since I normally leave the office around seven, I never have to deal with this stuff. It was stupid of me to forget that everybody else also gets off at five and are just as anxious to get home as I am.

Seriously, it should not take me over an hour to get home. Hopefully, Audrey is already there and able to pay for food delivery. Though, I would feel better if she would answer her damn text messages. It's not that hard and literally takes two seconds. I could message Tiffany, but I don't feel like dealing with her right now.

Finally, I pull into the parking garage and find my allotted spot. It's a tight squeeze because the asshole parked beside me obviously does not know how to stay between the lines. All I know is there better not be a fucking dent in my car when I come out here in the morning. Grabbing my bag, I rush out of the car and toward the elevators. Thank God it's working. Otherwise, I'd be walking up six flights of stairs and I really don't want to do that. Truth be told, the elevator was a selling point for me picking this apartment. I can't imagine carrying groceries up that many floors without losing something along the way.

I'm not surprised when the door to my apartment is unlocked. I can hear Tiffany and Audrey through the door before I even open it fully. If it was quiet, I would be worried. "Hey guys, I'm finally here."

They are sitting on the couch, glasses of wine in hand. Tiffany sets her glass on the coffee table and crosses her arms, glaring at me beneath her lashes. "Do I get to say I told you so now?" Her age really shows sometimes. Or, maybe it's because I'm exhausted from the insane drive home, but I'm not in the mood for her crap.

"You would be a lot less bitchy if you didn't." I knew she was going to have an attitude when I got here. If there's anything you can count on in regards to my youngest cousin, it's that she has some crazy mood swings. "Besides, it wasn't work that made me come home late. I forgot how stupid traffic is during rush hour. It should not have taken me that long to get home, considering I'm like fifteen minutes from the office."

"You probably could have walked and gotten here faster," Tiffany shrugs. "Oh well," she sighs. "Guess that means I can't give you a hard time."

I snort and then start choking on my own spit. Instead of helping me, she starts laughing. "You act like that's going to stop you."

"You have a point." She picks up her wineglass and takes a sip, dropping the subject...for now.

"Has the delivery guy shown up yet?" I look around the room and don't see any take out bags. Shit, maybe he got here before they did.

"Yup," Audrey replies. "It's all in the kitchen, and I paid using the emergency card you have hidden in your room."

"Thank you so much." My shoulders sag in relief, and the stress of the day washes away. "I was worried we'd be here with no food and have to go out for the night." I toss my bag on the coffee table and sit down between them. "I'm way too wiped out to go anywhere."

Audrey taps her finger against her chin. "You should probably put your emergency card somewhere else. The top drawer of your nightstand is pretty obvious, and it wasn't very well hidden."

She's always the sensible one, and the only person I know that puts so much thought into something like that. I slip the glass of wine from her hand and take a small drink. "You're probably right, but if I had put it somewhere else, you wouldn't have been able to pay the delivery guy."

"I have money of my own," she grumbles and takes back her glass.

"Can we eat now?" Tiffany is already standing up and walking toward the kitchen. "The food is getting cold."

"Do you always think with your stomach?" Audrey and I follow behind her. I'm only a few years older than her and I swear I can feel the pounds jumping onto my body just by smelling food. "You realize it can be reheated, right?"

"Yep," she laughs. "But it's better when it's fresh from the restaurant, and my stomach has never steered me wrong." She's unpacking the foil tins from the bag and the aroma of tomatoes and basil fill the room. "So, what is this news you wanted to tell us?"

"Let's wait until after we eat." Grabbing the plates from the cabinet, I slide them next to the lasagna. "Can you grab the bottle of wine?"

"Sure thing, Cuz." She skips off to the living room to get the bottle they opened earlier.

"Is whatever you're going to tell us going to send her into one of her temper tantrums?" Audrey nudges me aside to grab some silverware out of the drawer. "I just want to prepare myself if that's the case."

I shrug. It's all I can do, since I have no idea how Tiffany will react. "She might."

"Damn it," Audrey mutters. Seconds later her eyes widen and she plasters a big smile on her face as Tiffany enters the kitchen. "This smells delicious." Her subject change is terrible, but Tiffany doesn't seem to notice.

It sucks that we always have to tiptoe around things with Tiff. She's the baby of the family and tends to always get whatever she wants. You'd think since she's such a free spirit she would be okay with change, but that's not the case. Honestly, I think she'd lose her direction if it wasn't for Audrey and me keeping her somewhat steady. I blame it on my aunt and uncle. They indulged her way too much as a child. Hell, they still do it now. If she needs help making her rent payments, they give her the money. No questions asked. One day that girl is going to have to grow up, and she's going to fight it tooth and nail.

"Can you tell us now?" Tiffany's bouncing in her seat. Her red hair shifting slightly with the movement. No more wine for her, she gets way too hyper. "The suspense is killing me." Let's hope that excitement sticks around after she hears my news.

"I was offered a promotion," I squeal and clap my hands together. They pull me up from my chair, at the same time, and wrap their arms around me. We're all jumping up and down, unable to reign in the happiness radiating off of me.

"So, it looks like all of those ridiculously late nights you've been putting in have paid off," Tiffany laughs. "When do you get that big corner office and fat check?"

I withdraw from the group hug and wrap my arms around my waist. This is the part I've been leery of telling them. The dirty dishes capture my attention, and I focus on those instead of them. "Well, there might be a caveat to the whole promotion thing."

Tiffany's eyebrow lifts in question. Audrey throws her hand on her hip and stares me down. "What exactly do you have to do get this promotion?" I can't tell if that's worry or accusation behind her question.

They are already defensive, but I hope they don't flip their shit after they hear the rest. "First off, it is an amazing opportunity for me. So, you can wipe those ugly scowls off your faces." I hold up my index finger letting them know that I'm not finished. "Second, it will require me to relocate for a short period of time."

"What do you mean relocate?" Tiffany shrieks. "You can't just move because your boss wants you to. That's ridiculous."

I don't think I'm going to get her on board to do what I need to do in order to move up at my company. "People move for their jobs all the time. It's not anything new. Besides, it's not like I will be gone forever. A few months max. You will barely even notice that I'm gone."

Audrey cuts into the conversation before our younger cousin has a chance to go into full tirade mode. "Where will you be moving if you accept this offer?"

It's a good thing I did a little bit of research before telling them about the promotion. "It's this little town about 45 minutes south of Dallas. I've already checked to see how far away it is from here, and it's only about four hours."

"Four hours is an eternity," Tiffany cuts in groaning. "Do you really have to move?" Her shoulders slump.

"You traveled further than that when you followed me and Audrey to Austin. It's not that bad," I roll my eyes. "And yes, I have to if I want the promotion. And that's only if I get the distribution center up and running without a hitch."

"What does your direct boss think about it?" Audrey sits down, in full on adulting mode.

"Nothing good. He's not happy that Mr. Hart went

around him to ask me." I pour the last of the wine into my glass. "I think he wants me to fail so that I'll either be stuck where I am, or get canned."

"Your boss is an asshole," Tiffany deadpans. "I mean I'm not exactly happy about the prospect of you leaving for a few months, but I'm not hoping for you to fail. That would also make me an asshole."

"So, I have your support if I decide to take the offer?" Glancing at both of them, I take a drink of my wine. If they say no, I'm not sure what I'll do. They are my best friends, the ones I go to for everything. Even if I've been busy lately, I know despite their attitudes about it, they have my back. Tiffany paces back and forth in front of the kitchen sink, tapping her fingers on her thigh. "I mean, are you really worth a four-hour drive?" The dish towel from the table leaves my hand and sails through the air, hitting Tiff square in the face. "Damn, there's no need to be violent." She throws it back and knocks her glass over. Her aim is terrible. "Of course, we support you. I won't be jumping for joy when you aren't present for our weekly brunch, but I'm not so selfish that I would hold you back from your dream."

"That means a lot, Tiff. Thank you," I wrap my arms around her and give her a big squeeze. "Now, we should probably clean up the kitchen. I have to get some rest before I tell Mr. Hart my decision."

"Oh, man," Tiffany points to her wrist. "I have somewhere I need to be." She gives me a quick peck on the cheek, and rushes out of the apartment.

"You should have seen that coming," Audrey laughs. "I'll help you. And we'll come up with a game plan for when you move."

"Thanks," I mutter. "You know, your cousin really is an asshole."

"Last time I checked…she's your cousin, too."

She fills the sink with water as I gather the dishes off the table. "Yeah, I guess I'll claim her."

Chapter Five

My feet wobble in my heels as I make my way across the building to Mr. Hart's office. All of the other early birds stare at me. Their eyes wide, and whispers float through the mostly quiet room. I would be stupid to think it's not about me because I'm almost certain they've heard one version or another about my meeting yesterday. Maybe they've come up with their own speculations. Either way, I'm not a fan of being a part of the office gossip mill. It's never a good place to be, especially when it's typically fueled by jealousy.

I'm so focused on the jackholes I work with that I don't notice the small file box sitting on the floor. My shin crashes into the top, and I go sailing over the box. My hands slam against the floor, catching myself before my face eats tile. As if I wasn't already nervous, now we have my ungraceful fall in front of the entire office. Fuck my life. Honestly, I should come with a warning label-"will make an ass of herself at any given moment".

Slowly getting to my feet, I wipe my hands on my skirt. Tiny flecks of dirt and dust now cover my thighs. Proof that the office cleaning crew do not do a stellar job. Maybe I should bring that up with Mr. Hart while I'm in his office. Everyone should be disgusted at how dirty this floor is. Not to mention how nasty everything else must be.

I look up to see if anybody witnessed my epic crash. Of course, they saw me. Several of the guys have their hands over their mouths, attempting to hide their smirks and laughter. There were a few women just staring at me wearing shocked expressions. Not one of these jerks asked if I was okay. I swear, sometimes work is equivalent to being back in grade school. Except, people were a little more caring then.

"Don't worry everybody, I'm fine," I said feigning gratitude. Okay, so that was bitchy, but I don't really care.

Mr. Hart's office is mostly blocked by partitions, and today I am extremely grateful for that. His assistant, Rosie, is sitting behind her desk going through emails when I approach her. "Hey Rosie, is Mr. Hart in?"

"I'm sorry, Dear. He won't be in for another thirty minutes to an hour." She pauses in her scrolling, "What was that loud crash? Did somebody run into something? I swear some of the people out there are like bulls in a china shop."

My cheeks warm, and without looking in the mirror, I'm ninety percent sure they are bright red. "Actually," I sigh. "I'm the bull. I tripped over a stupid box and my face almost met the floor."

"Are you okay?" She rushes around her desk, puts her hands on my shoulders, checking me for injuries.

"I'm fine," I intend to nudge her away, but her mothering skills have taken over. There's no use trying to stop it. "The most I have is a nasty bruise on my leg where I hit the box."

Finally, she takes a step back looking at me with a questioning glance. "Well, if you're sure." Then, she walks around the desk to take a seat. "Do you want me to email you as soon as he comes into the office?"

Damn, I really wish he was here right now. I will have to deal with this nervous energy for at least another hour. "That would be great, Rosie. It's in regard to the meeting we had yesterday."

A sly smile takes over her face. "In that case, I'll push his other meetings back, and you will be the first person he speaks with." She winks at me, "This is a big opportunity for you, and I think you will do great." That woman knows everything that happens in this office. Hell, I'd be surprised if she didn't know everything that's going on in the entire building.

"Thanks." I give her a small wave, and head to my office. I guess I can work on whatever Mr. Granger emailed me late last night. As horrible as it is to say, I will definitely be happy not to be working so closely with him while I'm in Asheville.

There's a knock on my door and I stop filing. I've already gotten three paper cuts within a span of thirty minutes. Looking up, I gasp when I see who is standing in my doorway.

Why didn't Rosie let me know he was here? I would've gone to his office. It is weird seeing him on this side of the building, though. He must be impatient to hear my response.

"Did I startle you, Stella?" He takes a few steps toward my desk, and when he realizes there isn't an extra chair, he backs up and leans against the doorframe. He looks uncomfortable as his arms hang stiffly by his side.

"Sorry, Sir. I was expecting to meet you in your office." I glance around the room looking for something for him to sit on, but nothing magically appears in front of me. "Let me see if I can find an extra chair."

"Oh no, you don't have to go through all that trouble." He waves his hands in my direction. "I probably need to start taking more breaks to move around anyway."

It's weird having the head of the company standing without a place to sit. Finding an additional chair for my office has been bumped up on my list of priorities. "If you say so," I whisper. This is new territory for me, and I don't know how to navigate it.

"Rosie told me you were looking for me this morning. I take it you've made a decision about the relocation." He doesn't form it as a question so he has to know I've made a decision. I only hope it's the right one for me and my career. Only time will tell, I guess.

I clear my throat and place my hands on my desk to keep from fiddling with anything out of nerves. "Yes, Mr. Hart. I've decided I'd like to take the opportunity." I'm waiting for him to make a joke. To say he changed his mind, and he's sending Mr. Granger instead.

His hands smack together as he claps. "Excellent. I know you will do a fantastic job."

"I'm happy you have so much faith in me, and I will not let you down." His excitement is contagious, and I can't stop the wide grin from overtaking my lips. "When will I need to leave?" That's the one thing I forgot to ask when he first offered the possible promotion.

"Is two weeks enough time for you to get your affairs in order? If it is, I'll have Rosie call the rental property we found and let them know what your move-in date will be."

Damn, two weeks. I was expecting it to be more along the lines of a month, but the timeframe is doable. A mental list of everything that needs to happen forms in my mind. "Yes, two weeks is fine."

"Great," he taps the door frame with his knuckles. "I have a meeting in ten minutes, but I'll meet with you later this afternoon to discuss all of the arrangements." He turns to leave, and pauses with one foot out of the door. "You're going to go far in this company, Stella. This is only a stepping stone to get you where you want to be." He leaves without saying another word. My nerves are buzzing with excitement and nerves. *Can I do this?*

Two weeks. I'll be leaving the city that I love, and heading to a Podunk town. I hated going to these little towns in Nowheresville to visit family when I was a child. We were creative with how we spent our time, but Audrey and Tiffany were the only people that made the trip bearable. I will make the best of it, though. The prize at the end is more than worth it.

"Do you really need all of this stuff?" Tiffany sighs and she tapes up the last few boxes. It's probably more than I actually need, but I have no idea what there is to do in Asheville. I want to be prepared.

They should be proud of me; I never have my shit together like this. I grabbed one of the throw pillows off of my sofa and toss it at her head. She ducks and it goes sailing over her. She sticks her tongue out at me and continues taping the box in front of her.

"Yes, I need all of this. The house comes completely furnished, but that doesn't mean it also comes with my clothes, makeup, and shoes. A girl has to have options."

"It's not like you're going there to impress anybody," Audrey rolls her eyes. "You are there for one thing. To set up this center without a hitch, get your promotion, and get your ass back here so that we aren't lonely."

These two are ridiculous. They act like they'll never see me again. "And I'm going to do all that. However, I am allowed to have some downtime. We can totally do Sunday brunch over video while I am gone."

"It's not the same, though." Audrey folds her arms over her chest and her bottom lip pokes out. *Dramatic much?*

Good gravy, she's starting to act like Tiffany. I guess I didn't realize she would be so upset with me leaving. She's usually the practical one. "We will figure something out. Y'all can come visit me, and I will come back down here when I can."

"I guess," Audrey sighs and picks up one of the boxes. "I'm bummed we don't get to go down with you."

"I know, me too." I scrunch up my nose. "But I'm excited to check it out before y'all get there. What if I show up and the house is a dumpster fire?"

I wanted them to make the trip with me more than anything, but they couldn't get off work for two days to do it. Luckily, they will be there bright and early on Friday morning. It's the only day they were able to take off, or at least I hope they will.

Tiffany snorts. "You work for one of the best project

management companies in the city, there's no way they are going to put you in a crappy rental."

I hope she's right. I'm not sure what I would do if I walked up to my new temporary home and it was falling apart. Surely, Mr. Hart wouldn't do that. What am I saying? Mr. Hart most likely didn't set anything up. Most of that rests on Rosie's shoulders, and there's no way she would put me in a shady place. "We shall see." I grab one of the hair ties from the coffee table and throw my hair up in a ponytail. "Besides, I need to scope out some places we can hang out before y'all get there Friday morning."

"That's what I'm talking about," Tiffany laughs. "Finally! You have your priorities on the right path."

My apartment looks weird and bare. All the big stuff is still in place, but all the little touches that make the space my own are packed away so that I have a little bit of home with me while I'm gone. "Y'all are going to come check on the apartment while I'm gone, right? You don't have come over here daily, but once or twice a week to get the mail and make sure nobody realizes I'm not here would be amazing."

"We got you, sister." I love that she uses that term. It's something her mom has said since we were kids. It didn't matter which of us she was talking to, she always called us sister. And it works. These two, even though they are my cousins, feel like my sisters. They're the first to know anything and everything going on in my life. It's a bond that I hope never breaks. "Who knows, maybe I'll come stay here a couple of nights to get away from my crazy roommate. I really need a screening process the next time around." Tiffany has an evil grin on her face, and I don't trust it.

Pointing my finger at her, as if I'm scolding her, I shake

my head. "No random dudes in my apartment. You can have whatever sexcapades you want in your own bed. Just don't do it here."

She gasps and covers her chest with her hand. "I would never do that."

Audrey crosses her arms over her chest. "Oh really? What about that time you practically had sex in front of me, or when you used my car and I found a condom wrapper in the backseat?" She pulls one arm away and points it at Tiffany. "You better get that agreement in writing. Or, do I need to count off all the other ways you have been irresponsible when it comes to men?"

"I was practically a kid when all that happened," she argues. "You can't hold what I did a million years ago against me forever. Besides, I'm not currently dating anyone right now. I'm only trying to avoid the roommate from hell."

"I'm trusting you, Tiff." This is going to bite me in the ass. I can already feel it. "Please don't let me down. Anyway, what's going on with your roommate?"

"I won't, I promise." She picks up the box holding all of my bathroom stuff. Deflection at its finest. I actually like her roommate, well as much as I can since I rarely see her. She keeps things tidy and organized. She's also the exact opposite of Tiffany. "Let's get some of the crap you're going to need loaded into your car. I'm sure you'll want to get an early start."

Each of us grabs a box. I can't believe I'm doing this. Tomorrow morning, I will begin a new adventure, and it terrifies me. My cousins better be there to catch me if this whole thing blows up in my face.

Chapter Six

FINALLY, a freaking gas station. I'm barely an hour out of Austin, and I already have to pee. Reason number one why I shouldn't drink a ton of water before a long drive. I'm shocked I haven't had to stop sooner. Tiffany and Audrey always make fun of me for my frequent stops. It got to the point where they wouldn't let me have anything to drink before a trip. They call me a time suck, and treat me like a child. At least, I stay hydrated and won't have a ton of wrinkles when I'm older. Point one for me.

I exit the highway and drive toward the gas station mentioned on the sign. Nothing has gone according to plan today. I woke up late after too many glasses of wine with the girls, completely missing the five alarms I had set. It may be overkill but I'm not a morning person and it takes some motivation to get my ass out of bed. Too bad it doesn't always work.

On top of that, Mr. Granger called and needed me in the office as soon as possible because he needed help with something. I won't even mention that it was something anyone in the office could've helped him with. My best guess is that he was doing everything he possibly could to delay my departure. I don't understand why this man wants me to fail so badly. I've never done something to disappoint him, at least I don't think I have. Each task he's set before me, I've completed on time and perfectly. Well, except that report fiasco a few weeks ago. That wasn't timely or perfect.

Let's just say this adventure is starting off rocky. Now I probably won't get to my destination until well after dark. I should have just waited and headed there with Audrey and Tiffany on Friday morning. Damn it, I shouldn't have drank with them last night. Peer pressure, man. It'll get me every time.

Now I'm sitting outside of this creepy ass gas station debating whether or not I have to pee that bad. The paint is peeling off the building. The front door has a thick coating of dust, and the open sign flickers on and off erratically. If I was with someone, I would suck it up and go inside. But I'm alone and the building gives me skeevy vibes. I'm going with my gut, and back out of the parking lot.

There is another gas station, that I know is amazing, a little further along the highway. At least there, I know the bathroom will be clean. It's what the gas station is known for, and they just so happen to be place strategically along the two major highways that run North to South. Well, that and being the size of a grocery store with a ton of cute things lining their shelves, and what seems like a million gas pumps. The other plus side…fountain Big Red, need I say more? The only problem I foresee is spending too much time, and money, in there while perusing all the stuff they have for sale. Maybe I will find something for Tiffany and Audrey to thank them for helping me. They didn't have to go out of their way, and take off work, to help me realize my goals. Even though they did their fair share of complaining about it.

Does everyone around here drive this slow on the highway? The worst part is it's only two lanes and I'm blocked in from all sides. It's going to take me forever to get used to this pace. Back in Austin, the motto is "go fast or get run over". This is one of the reasons I rarely visit my aunts and uncles. The slower pace feels like I'm moving at snail speed.

That isn't the only reason, though. The mere thought of staying in a tiny town for longer than necessary gives me hives. There's nothing to do except sit around at the kitchen table, or on the porch, and share the family gossip. I have to admit that it's not all bad. I've heard some crazy stories about my dad and aunts. It's just not my idea of a good time. All you do is sit and drink. There aren't any clubs or fun places to visit.

The British voice on my GPS blares through the speakers, and I jump, almost swerving off the road. They should really ease into the old voice so you have some warning. Something like those alarms that start off quietly and slowly build in volume until it's yelling at you to get out of bed. Maybe I need one of those alarms. My exit is in two miles, and I'm really hoping this car in front of me doesn't take the same one.

The Asheville city limits sign catches my eyes as I take the ramp on the service road. Lights fill the streets and cars are moving along at a steady pace. A coffee shop sits on the corner, and I feel my first moment of relief. A few of the stores I shop at back home can be seen dotting the busy road. Maybe it won't be so bad here after all. They have coffee and decent stores. I couldn't ask for much else.

The town lights are now only a reflection in my rearview mirror. I should have looked at the address to my rental house more closely. It appears I won't be staying in town, close to everything I could ever need. Nope. My phone is leading me straight to the middle of nowhere. *Damn it*. Next time I'm asked to relocate, I'm going to have to get with Rosie on the specifics. I assumed I would be in a nice apartment with a ton of pain in the ass neighbors. That's apparently not the case.

I haven't seen a house in over a mile, and forget about street lights. What in the world did I do to piss off Rosie so badly? There's no way she would have put me in the boonies without a reason. I'm going to call her first thing in the morning to see what the hell she was thinking when she picked this place.

My phone rings and the lit-up screen distracts me for a split second. It's Audrey, and I know she's expecting to talk to me tonight. I raise my hand to press the accept call button but jerk it away when a dark shape darts out into the road in front of me. I freak out and swerve, screaming, right into a ditch. The car groans and shakes as it comes to a jolting stop. I look back to see what kind of animal it was, but it's gone. As if it never existed. A loud hiss comes from the hood, and I groan. That doesn't sound promising. *Damn it*. I just bought this car.

Chapter Seven

NO SIGNAL. I sigh in defeat as I will the service bars to show up on my phone. *Just freaking great.* Today officially wins for the suckiest day ever.

This relocation is already proving to be a huge mistake. I should have turned around the second my headlights met darkness. I bring the phone closer to my face, inspecting the map that is still on the screen. It doesn't look like there are any houses close to the one I'll be staying in. If I ever get there. It's completely isolated. I feel like I am in one of those eighties' horror movies. The ones where the dumb girl runs through the woods, barely dressed, and gets axed in the end.

Why did I say yes to this? I'm sitting here, in the ditch, completely stranded. *Son of a bitch.* Whatever it was that derailed my attempt to see my new temporary home was too small to be a dog, but too big to be a rabbit. I hope wherever it is, it's grateful that I didn't plow over it. Not that I would do anything intentionally, but I've seen my fair share of roadkill littering the road. Either way, there's no telling how much damage is now done to my car. My poor baby, she's barely two months old. I run my hand across the dashboard, trying to soothe the pain of an inanimate object, or maybe I am just trying to comfort myself. Either way, I feel a little bit better. If I don't get this car running, there's no way I'm going to be able to get back and forth from the distribution center now. What the fuck am I going to do?

Headlights shine in my rearview mirror. Finally, someone is coming down this stupid road. Maybe they will be the rescuer I desperately need right now. I have no idea how I'm going to get out of this predicament on my own since I can't get any cell reception in this spot. Otherwise, I would have called AAA. Hopefully cell signal isn't an issue at the house. I need a way to talk to my best friends so they can talk me off the deep end when I want to throw in the towel.

If I can't get this person to stop, the only other option I have is to get out of my car and walk until I can find someone who will help me. In the dark, with the moon as my only source of light. On the plus side, the road doesn't look like it sees a ton of traffic. What am I even thinking about here? If I wouldn't pee at a gas station that looked creepy, there's no way in hell I'm going to willingly traipse off into the dark alone. Like I said before, that's just a bad horror movie waiting to happen.

Seconds pass as I watch the headlights get closer and a truck fly by me. Suddenly, the driver slam on the brakes. At least that means they saw me. Now, let's see if they decide to help or drive off like so many other drivers do in the city. The truck door swings open and a boot clad foot steps onto the ground. It seems as if they might be dressed to help me out of this sticky situation.

I can't really see who has come to my rescue since my

headlights are facing the grassy hill at an awkward angle. But from the light glow of the moon, I can make out a tall figure with the frame of a man. I'm trying not to swoon and act like a damsel in distress, but his broad stature makes me want to see what he looks like up close.

I watch the man walk toward my car, trying to wipe images of serial killers out of my mind. His strides are long, steady, and confidence pours off of him. When his knuckles tap against the window, I roll it down. Thankful that at least this feature is still working. Even if he's here to help, I don't want to get out of the car until I know I'm not going to be chopped up into tiny pieces. Self-preservation is something I've learned after living in the city my entire life. Nobody has ever approached me, but that doesn't mean I shouldn't be prepared at all times.

He bends down until we are face to face. "Are you okay?" His voice is deep and holds a bit of a southern twang. His voice breaks the nighttime soundtrack of crickets and other creatures I can't identify. I need to know if his appearance matches the octave of his voice. It's a sound I could definitely get used to, and it doesn't sound like he could be a potential serial killer.

Lifting my hand over my head to the roof of my car, I search for the button to turn on the interior light, without losing eye contact with my rescuer. My finger hits the right button, and I squint my eyes as my car is illuminated. Going from dark to light is always a pain, and it takes a moment for my eyes adjust. My mouth falls open. The scruff on his face is hotter than it should be, and his dark brown eyes hold a spark in the dim car light. He is the exact opposite of anyone I have ever been interested in, and yet there is something about him. I have to remind myself that I'm only here for a small amount of time. I do not need to find the locals attractive.

"Miss?" A tinge of worry is laced in the question. "Are you alright?"

"Oh," I shake the lustful thoughts out of my head. "Yes, I'm fine. Well," I laugh nervously. "As fine as I can be, considering..." I wave my hand in a wide arc to include my predicament.

"Do you want me to look at your car and see if I can figure out what is wrong with it, or if it can be driven?" He seems genuine but then again so did Ted Bundy.

"Uh, sure." What else am I supposed to say? Calling anyone is out, and he's the first person I've seen come down this road in the past hour. "Can I help?" It's not like I'd be able to help with anything remotely car related. My dad wasn't one of those to teach me how to work on vehicles. We always took our cars to a mechanic. He said it was because he spent his entire teen years covered in grease, constantly fixing whatever happened to go awry in his old beat up truck. He didn't want that for me.

"No, I've got it. I just need to go back to my truck for a flashlight."

I turn toward the passenger seat for my purse, but the contents are scattered all over the floor. "I'm sure I have one in he—" When I face the window again, he's already gone, jogging to his truck. And I'm left talking to air. I didn't realize he meant right this second.

My mystery rescuer doesn't come back to the window. Instead, he clicks the flashlight on and begins inspecting my car. The deep frown on his face does not bode well for me. He goes a step further and gets down on the ground to look for damage underneath. The amount of time he's taking makes me nervous, and I wonder how I'm going to get to my destination if I can't drive the car. Maybe this is a sign that I need to get back to Austin as fast as I can. I am obviously not meant for country living.

His head pops above the hood of my car, and I jump. I need to lay off the scary movies. They're making me jump at every sudden movement, and if this place is as remote as it seems…I'll end up completely freaking myself out. He's back at my window and running his hands through his wavy locks. "Um, I don't think it's a good idea for you to drive it." He doesn't turn his flashlight off, and it shines right in my face. I squint my eyes from the brightness. When he notices, he points the light toward the ground. "I have a chain in the back of my truck, and I can tow it to your house tonight, if you want."

Leaving my new baby on the side of the road probably isn't a smart idea. There isn't anything in here that I'm worried about being stolen, it's just the car itself. I don't know anybody here, and I'm not sure what might happen if it is left unattended. "Yeah, that would be great." I hold my hand out of the window, "I'm Stella, by the way."

"I'm Johnny," he places his hand in mine. Calluses brush against my palm, and I'm a little surprised that I like the way it feels. Most of the guys I've held hands with work in offices and have no reason to have roughened hands. He pulls his hand away. "You're pretty trusting considering you're stuck in the middle of nowhere, and broken down. How do you know you can trust me?" He smirks, and leans back away from the window. His face now hidden in shadows, and I can't stop the shiver that runs through my body. This man is going to be trouble, I can already tell.

"I don't really have much of a choice," I shrug. "It's either sit out here in the dark by myself. Or, trust that you aren't some deranged serial killer." Even though he has definitely captured my attention, he hasn't set off my creep radar yet. It's so hard to find genuinely nice men these days. *Calm down, Stella.* He's only being a good Samaritan.

"Don't worry, I'm not a serial killer." He chuckles at my arched eyebrow. "Where do you live? I don't think I've seen you around here before, and I know everyone in this town." Damn, if he knows I'm an outsider, this town must be pea size.

I rattle off the address Rosie gave me. Johnny's nose scrunches at me in confusion. "I just moved here, and I was on my way to the house, when something ran out in the road and I ended up here. So, I'm not exactly sure where my house is." I feel like a complete dumbass for not knowing, but it's not my fault. This is why I wanted to get here during the day. But no, Mr. Granger had to ruin that for me.

"I know where it's at." He looks over my car and shakes his head. "It's the old Garnett place. Nobody has lived there in years, but it has a very narrow and twisty driveway, and I don't know if I can safely get your car down it in the dark."

Great, the news just gets better and better. The way he said the name of the house makes me think it's not even livable. I am seriously questioning what exactly I got myself into. Mr. Hart said my accommodations were nice and completely furnished. I hope that's true because I don't have anything with me, besides my clothes, shoes, and the essentials I'll need in the morning. Audrey and Tiffany won't be here with the rest of my crap until tomorrow. "Are there any other options that don't include me leaving my car on the side of the road?"

Johnny taps his chin, considering my question. "There

is one, but I'm not sure how keen you are on going to a stranger's house. Other than that, it's leaving it here until you can get a tow truck."

Normally, it would be an automatic no if someone asked me to come to their house. Especially if I've just met them. But I'm sick of being in this car and feel gross from driving all day. Not to mention, I'm hungry. All of those points lead to me saying, "It depends on who the stranger is."

Chapter Eight

I'VE BEEN BANISHED to Johnny's truck. He wouldn't let me help with anything. I tried, and he sounded more frustrated than anything else. He even grabbed the few bags, and suitcases, I brought with me, and put them in the backseat. I mean, I'm not one of those people that thinks I need to do everything myself, but I'm fully capable of carrying my own stuff. Either he thinks I'm a nuisance, or he's a true gentleman. I'm not sure which, yet.

My hands reach forward, inches away from opening the glove compartment. The urge to go through his things to see what type of man he is overpowering me. I snatch them back before I go into spy mode. Here Johnny is, helping me out of a bind, and my first instinct is to snoop. I'm such a shitty human being.

The windows are rolled down, and a slight breeze comes through them. It doesn't help much. It's still crazy hot even though it's the middle of September. I hear grunts and groans coming from behind the truck, and I look in the side view mirror to see what the problem is. All I see is darkness. "Are you okay? Do you need any help?"

Johnny's head pokes out from behind the tailgate. "Nope. I'm good. I only need a couple more minutes and we'll be on the road."

"Suit yourself," I mutter under my breath. It would probably go a lot faster if I was out there helping him. Not sitting in the truck with nothing to do. Oh well, his loss.

I grab my phone from my purse and move it around in all directions. Still no service. I don't understand how this is possible with the amount of cell towers there are everywhere. It's a good thing I'm not in imminent danger. I'd be royally screwed. Luckily, I have a few games I can play without a connection. Seriously, anything to kill time is better than sitting in the cab of this truck, alone, with nothing to do.

The driver side door opens and Johnny slides in behind the wheel. Of course, the one game I'm trying to play needs an update. Can't do that without a damn signal. I throw the phone onto the seat beside me, and it hits with a dull thud. "Please tell me there is a signal somewhere in this town. I can't deal with being cut off from everything."

He shakes his head and smirks. "Yeah, there is. Most of the time you have to have a certain carrier in order for your phone to work flawlessly." He shrugs his shoulders and turns on the truck. "It's one of the downfalls of living out here."

"Well that's promising." I face the window and stare into the darkness. It's really going to suck if I can't talk to the girls on a daily basis. They are my only connection to my normal life. To home. I should have said no when Mr. Hart offered me the job. I have a sinking feeling that my stay here will be one big ball of suck.

Johnny taps his fingers against the steering wheel, adding a steady rhythm into the quiet stillness. It's soothing and annoying at the same time. I'm not sure how that's possible, but it's like my own personal hell right now. I just want to be home in my comfortable bed, listening to Audrey and Tiffany bicker over a video call.

"So, what brings you this way?" His deep voice breaks the silence, and his fingers are no longer moving.

I eye him warily, unsure if I should answer. "A temporary relocation for my job. Though, I'm starting to regret the decision after the crappy night I've had." I continue staring outside, attempting to take in the scenery, and my surroundings, with only the light the moon is producing. Too bad there are so few out tonight. "Why? Are you trying to make sure I don't have anybody looking for me?"

He laughs so hard the truck swerves the tiniest bit. "I figured that would be the last of your concerns considering you got in the truck with me. But no, I'm just trying to make friendly conversation. Getting to know your neighbors is important in areas like this. We're all like family and look out for each other."

I look him up and down, deciphering the truth behind his words. Surely if he was going to do something horrible, he wouldn't have hooked my car up to his truck. "It's so different in the city. Most of the time when the people in my apartment building see each other they do their best to avoid each other at all costs. It's not exactly a super friendly environment."

I keep searching for store fronts, anything to make this place feel like something more than a forgotten space. "Wow, there really isn't anything out here is there?"

"Not really. We have a small convenience store, but that's about it." He has one hand on the wheel, and scratches the back of his neck with the other. Is he ashamed, or at a loss for words? "You will have to drive a good fifteen to twenty minutes to get to any big grocery stores, and an hour to get to Dallas." That's definitely not what I want to hear. Driving isn't an issue for me, but I'm used to the store being a couple of blocks away. I honestly don't even remember the last time I actually went to the grocery store. Most of the time I get them delivered, or eat out.

"Why in the hell would they choose to build a distribution center out here?" I mutter under my breath. Hopefully he can't hear me. I truly can't fathom the thought process behind corporate's decision, but who am I to question their decisions.

We pull off the road onto what I assume is a driveway. I can't really tell because there aren't any lights. He pulls to a stop in front of a small, older looking house. "I assume this is your house?"

"Yup," he shifts the truck into park. "If you want, you can hang out inside while I move your car to the garage. I can have the shop I work for pick it up in the morning."

I look from the house to him, and nod. "That would be great." Stretching my arms over my head, I sigh at the thought of being in a much bigger space. "Being in a car all day has my arms and legs so freaking stiff. Walking around, and stretching my muscles, is probably a good idea."

Before I even have a chance to pull the door handle, he's out of the truck, and opening the door for me. I flinch. Not out of fear or anything, but because this is not something I experience often. As soon as I'm out of the truck, he reaches into the backseat and pulls out a pizza and pack of beer. I didn't even know those were back there. Maybe that's why he wanted to put my bags in the truck. He didn't want to chance me ruining his dinner.

"I'll unlock the door for you. I have pizza." He lifts it up as if I didn't just see him pull it out of the truck. "And I'm sure there's something to drink in the refrigerator. I'm not sure if the beer is any good anymore. It's been sitting in the heat for longer than I anticipated." I follow him to the door, and walk in behind him. "Help yourself. It shouldn't take me too long to get your car unhooked from my truck."

"Thanks," I smile as he sets the pizza on the counter. "I really appreciate your help."

"No problem. I'll be right back." He walks quickly out of the house, like something is lighting his shoes on fire. Did I do something to offend him? I have no idea what is going on with him. I tried flirty banter, and he basically shut me down. Now he's acting like a teenager that doesn't know how to be in the same room as girl.

I'm beginning to think there's something wrong with me. I can't manage to capture a guy's attention long enough to do anything about it. Or…maybe it's him. He may not be all that great with women. I guess time will tell, not that I'm looking for someone to date. I have a job to do.

As he'll be occupied for a few minutes, it's time to do some snooping. The best place to accomplish that is the bathroom. What people keep in their cabinets is always a good indicator of what's going on in their life.

Chapter Nine

THIS CANNOT SERIOUSLY BE HAPPENING. First the car, then no phone signal, and now this...what did I do to someone in a past life to deserve the shit storm my day has been? Getting my foot out of the damn hole should not be this hard. Johnny standing in the entryway laughing his ass off isn't helping. I thought he was a gentleman. This isn't how people treat guests in their house.

"How did you manage to do that? I have all the plates and stuff on the counter for the pizza." Johnny asks between gasps. I really don't think it's that funny.

"I needed to wash my hands." It's a lie, but he doesn't need to know that. I was snooping. How else was I going to establish once and for all that he didn't have ill intentions? As far as I can tell, this guy is pretty clean. That's almost unheard of in today's world. Everyone has dirt, including me. I'm sure there are photos from high school somewhere online of me making a complete ass of myself. I happen to think I'm perfectly normal, for the most part, anyway. I guess I'll have to do more digging. There *has* to be some skeletons hiding in his closet.

"Sure, you were," he mutters under his breath, and grabs my outstretched hand. "You might want to turn your foot to the left, or it's going to get caught on the wood. I'm sure that would hurt a hell of a lot more than your ego does right now."

"Ugh," I roll my eyes. I listen to him, though. I shift my foot to the left and point my toe. He pulls me up and I fall into his arms, completely unbalanced. His fingers graze my back under my shirt, and linger for longer than necessary. "Thank you," I pull away from him, and his smirk, and rub my hands down my shirt, smoothing out fake wrinkles. My gaze falls on his mouth, still grinning at my stupidity. *Stop it*. I need to stop checking him out. He's hot as hell, but I do not have time in my life for men. Not today, tomorrow, or ever. I came to this Podunk town to do one thing, my job. As soon as it's done, I'll be driving my happy little ass right back to Austin. Johnny reaches around me and grabs the pizza box, flipping the lid open. "You didn't eat?" He looks from the pizza to me. "Do you not like pizza?"

"I like pizza just fine," I huff. "It's rude to eat when the person who bought it isn't eating at the same time." I hope that's a thing because right now I'm talking out of my ass. I spent the ten minutes it took him to unhook my car snooping through his bathroom and living room. I was just about to go through his kitchen cabinets when I heard a loud clang. The sound was loud, and scared the hell out of me. Hence, my foot falling into the hole. I stare the hole down as if it's wronged me somehow, and I guess it did. That's beside the point, though. "What's up with floor?" I nod toward it.

"It was weak," he picks up a slice of pizza and takes a bite. Cheese comes off in strands and covers his chin. It's kind of adorable. Stop it, brain. "I fell through it last night. I have all the stuff to fix it, and was actually going to do it tonight, until…" He waves his pizza in my direction, letting the sentence hang.

Until my driving mishap. I'm grateful for his help, but he doesn't have to rub it in. It's not like I sought out an animal running across the road.

Something in his pocket vibrates, and I look down. As much as I don't want to admit my attraction to him, a small part of me wonders who might be calling him, and my heart sinks a little at the thought of it being another woman. Wait a minute, that's my phone. "What are you doing with my phone?" I pluck it out of his pocket, but the Pop Socket on the back gets caught on the fabric and I accidentally pull him closer to me.

Johnny has enough foresight to set the pizza on the counter before helping me with my phone. His cheeks are a bright red, and knowing that I affect him makes me smile. At least I'm not the only one who is flustered. "Um, you left it in my truck when you got out, and it started ringing when I drove your car to the barn."

"Okay." My cousins have been blowing up my phone. There are so many notifications they don't all fit on the home screen preview. "But why did you have it in your pocket?"

He shrugs, and takes a step back. "I figured you might want it now that you have cell reception." Another step back. He's putting distance between us, and I can't tell if it's because he's scared of me and how I might react. Or, because he thinks I'm too much. It's not an inaccurate observation. I've been told many times that I'm high maintenance, even though I don't see it.

"Oh, well," my voice is shaky and breathless. Shit, he's really going to think I'm crazy if I keep going back and forth like this with my mood. It's not something I'm doing on purpose, but he's throwing me off my game. Add in the events of tonight, it's no wonder I'm flustered. "Thank you. I appreciate it."

My phone vibrates in my hand, and I almost drop it. "No problem." He nods toward my hand, "You might want to get that. It sounds like whoever is trying to call you won't give up until you answer." Is that a frown? Maybe he thinks I have a boyfriend badgering me and he's upset about it. A girl can wish.

Instead of answering, I decline the call and pull up my text messages.

Stella: I can't talk right now. I'll fill you in soon.
Audrey: What? Why not?
Tiffany: You aren't doing something stupid are you? And if you are...wait for me!
Stella: Don't worry about it. I will call y'all in less than two hours.

Pressing the button on the side of my phone, I turn it off. Otherwise, those two will keep texting and calling until I give them an answer they deem appropriate. They drive me insane sometimes.

"Is everything okay?" Johnny puts his hand on my shoulder. It's heavy, warm, and comforting. I didn't even notice him move closer to him. I have to stop zoning out, especially when I'm with someone I don't know.

"Yeah. It's just my cousins being worrywarts." My stomach growls, reminding me that I haven't eaten dinner.

"Any chance I can get a slice of that pizza before you take me to my new house?"

He uses the hand that was on my shoulder to pick up the box, and I would almost rather him touch me than eat. There's a spark I've never felt before, even if he thinks I'm a moron for going off the road. "Of course. I told you to eat before I went outside."

"I was a bit distracted," I wave his statement off.

"I'm sure," he mumbles. Was I meant to hear that? I have a feeling he knows exactly what I was doing while he was outside. This is mortifying.

"On second thought," I grab a couple of slices of pizza and set them on a paper plate. "Can you take me now? I can eat on the way."

If I had to describe the driveway we pull into, it would be creepy as hell. Overgrown trees line the path on both sides, and it doesn't give me much hope for the condition of the house. It reminds me of those haunted houses they show on TV with the spooky landscapes overlaying the image of the house. Add in the fact that it's the middle of the night…and we have nailed the creep factor to a level ten.

"This driveway is extremely long," I say into the quiet cab. There has been zero talking since we got in. So, what if it's been less than five minutes? Some conversation is better than nothing. "Are we almost there?"

"Yes," he points into the darkness. "It's just around the next curve."

This driveway has way more curves than absolutely necessary. Who were these people that built this house?

It's pretty far off the road, hidden behind a copse of trees, and a nightmare to get to. I'm only hoping that everything is functioning, and nothing is falling apart.

My eyes widened as soon as the house comes into view. It's not a worn down, shabby dwelling like I assumed it might be. No, it's everything a small-town girl could dream of. There are two floors, and I can't tell because it's dark, but I think the porch wraps all the way around. I'm bouncing in my seat, anxious to see what the inside looks like. "When you said old Garnett house, I assumed you meant it was going to be completely run down."

He laughs, "That's what you get for assuming." He pulls the truck right in front of the house, and puts it in park. "I'm not sure who's been taking care of it, but I think they've done some remodeling on the inside. This used to be the house where everyone in town would gather for cookouts and any sort of event. Mr. and Mrs. Garnett didn't have any kids, and I thought it was abandoned until a few years ago."

"Really?" My level of excitement has just gone up a few notches. If this house is as amazing on the inside as it is on the outside, it may not be so awful living here until the job is done.

Johnny nods, and unbuckles his seat belt. "Do you need help with your bags?"

I completely forgot about the duffel bags he set in the back seat before attaching my car to his truck with a chain. I won't even talk about how weird that looked. I could easily take them in myself, but I don't know that I want to go into this new place alone. What if the inside is a total shit show? Or worse…haunted. "Sure, I'll grab one and you grab the other?" Grabbing the door handle before he has a chance to come around, I swing the door open. I step down from the truck, and peer up at the house. This is either going to be awesome, or go up in flames. Either way, it's my home for the time being.

Chapter Ten

Sweat forms between my hand and the bag I'm carrying, and my steps are clumsy as I walk up the stairs to the front door of my new home. Gently setting down my bag, I bend to pull the key out from under the mat. I breathe a sigh of relief when I feel the warm metal meet my fingertips. It was right where Rosie said it would be in the email she sent me with all the information. Deep breath in, and out. As I slip the key into the doorknob, I don't move my hand. This is a big moment. Not because I've never been on my own. It's just that I've never been this far away from my family. *How am I supposed to adult without them?*

"Do you need some help?" Johnny's voice behind scares the hell out of me. For a second, I forgot he was here. This man I don't even know has been a witness to the insanity of my life today. He must think I'm a moron.

I shake my head. I will not show weakness to this stranger. Even if he is attractive. "No, I'm sorry. I sort of spaced out for a second." There's no sense in delaying the inevitable. This is my life, for now, and I need to pull up my big girl panties and deal with it. I turn the key, pull it out and place it in my pocket. I'll need to put it on a keyring so I don't chance losing it in the future. Placing my hand back on the knob, I give it a small twist. The door opens, creaking with every inch. "Is it supposed to do that?"

"It's an old house," Johnny shrugs. "No matter how much remodeling has been done, it's likely to show its age in small ways."

Nodding, I pick up my bag and take a step inside. He follows right behind me. My hand finds the wall, feeling around for the light switch. There's no way I'm going a step further without a way to see what's around me. Finally, I find the switch, and the foyer is illuminated. My eyes adjust from the dark to the sudden brightness, and I gasp.

Johnny runs towards me. "Is everything okay? Is there something awful in here?" He's such a gentleman, and I can't wrap my head around why he'd be so kind to me. A woman he's never met before this night.

"No," I shake my head. "It's stunning." My eyes are tearing up at the sheer beauty of this house. He moves around me until his dark brown eyes meet mine. "Absolutely breathtaking." I'm not sure anymore if I'm talking about him, or the house. Either way, I'm in complete awe.

I clasp my hands together and turn in circles, taking in the entire room. "My cousins are never going to want to leave." Seeing this house has completely turned my day around. It's still a pretty shitty day, but this makes it absolutely worth it.

"I think I'm going to go," Johnny says quietly.

"Sorry," I cover my mouth. "I forgot you were here for a moment." Again…he doesn't need to know that, though. I'm such a horrible person for pushing him out of my mind so easily. It's not easy to do, considering he helped me out, and I keep checking him out every chance I get.

"It's all good," he says. "I'm glad your night seems to have turned around." He takes a couple of steps backward toward the door. "I'm going to find something to write my number on so you can call me in the morning. In case you need a ride, or help figuring out what to do about your car." He adds that last bit in a rush. I make him nervous, and I'm not sure how I feel about that. He seems like a genuinely nice guy, and someone I can see myself spending time with while I'm here. As friends only, I tell myself. You do not have time for any flings.

"Tiffany and Audrey should be here early in the morning, so I shouldn't need a ride anywhere. But I'll definitely call about the car. She's my brand-new baby." I practically run toward him, and wrap him in a hug. "Thank you for stopping tonight. I didn't think anyone was going to come to my rescue and I'd be left walking down a dark road to find help."

"You're welcome?" His voice goes up an octave, nowhere near the deep, sexy tone he had moments ago. Oh shit, did I make things weird? It wasn't my intention, but I felt like a hug was an appropriate gesture. And, I got to feel his body against mine. It's been so long since I've embraced someone other than my family.

I release my hold on him, giving him a slight chance of running away, frightened by the crazy blonde lady. He doesn't move. I pull my phone out of my back pocket and hold it toward him. "Here." Shoving it in his hands I back up, putting some distance between us. "Just put your number in my phone to make things easier. I never carry pen and paper with me. My entire life is in the palm of your hand right now. I'd be lost without it."

"Okay," he taps on my phone and hands it back to me. "I guess I'll talk to you tomorrow. If you need anything, don't hesitate to call. I'm less than five minutes away."

"Will do," I nod. "Goodnight Johnny. And really, thank you for everything." I walk him toward the door, and wave when his foot hits the bottom step. Watching him walk away isn't a bad view. His jeans hug him in all the right places, and I tamp down the little voice in my head telling him to come back. It's crazy to feel such a strong attraction to someone I've just met, right?

My phone is in my hand before he pulls out of the driveway, calling my cousins, as I'm making my way up the stairs to find my bedroom.

"It's about freaking time," Tiffany yells. "You were supposed to be there hours ago."

"I know," I sigh. "You wouldn't believe the day I've had. I had to stop to pee. And when I finally got here, something ran out in front of me, and I ended up in a ditch."

"Oh my gosh," Audrey whispers. "Are you okay?"

"Yeah, I'm fine. My car, not so much." I rub my forehead with my free hand, and plop onto the bed of what I assume is the master bedroom. It's definitely spacious with plenty of room to walk around. Hell, I could work out in here if I really wanted to. That's crazy talk, though. All I want to do right now is curl up in this blanket and pass out.

"This is why you need to go home with us more often. You have no idea how to drive on country roads." Tiffany chastises me. She's not normally the one who gripes me out about things like this. Maybe my absence is making her realize she needs to grow up. At least a little bit.

"If your car is messed up, how did you get to the house?" Audrey voice is full of suspicion.

"A guy stopped to help me. He fed me and gave me a ride. He even helped me get the car off the road."

"Are you insane?" Ah, my sensible cousin always ready to talk to me about the dangers of being out in the world alone. "He could have been a horrible person and hurt you."

"But he wasn't," I deadpan. "And I didn't want to sit around waiting for someone else to help. I didn't have any signal where it happened."

"That's why the call dropped when I was trying to call you," Tiffany says.

"Bingo." I move until my head finds the pillows. They are old and lumpy, but the thought of going back downstairs to get the bag holding my pillows is too much of a nuisance. "What time are y'all heading out in the morning?"

"We'll talk about this when we get there," Audrey whisper yells. She never raises her voice too much no matter how angry she is. "And we're leaving here around six thirty, and should be there around ten. Maybe sooner."

"You are lucky I love you," Tiffany pipes in. "That's entirely too early for me to wake up unless I have work."

"You'll be fine," I mutter. "Anyway, I'm pretty wiped out. I'm going to head to bed. I'll see y'all tomorrow. Love you."

"Love you, too," they chorus, and the line goes dead.

I set the alarm on my phone and place it on the table next to the bed. I'm not used to being surrounded by all this quiet. It'll be a miracle if I fall asleep at a decent time.

Chapter Eleven

I WAKE up minutes before my alarm goes off. There is absolutely no reason to be up before seven when my cousins are probably just now hitting the road. I know Audrey said they'd be leaving at six thirty, but let's be honest, there's no way they walked out of my apartment until probably right now. I know Tiffany too well.

First thing on the agenda, a shower. I feel gross from traveling yesterday, and after a rough night of sleep, I need to wash away my worries. I run downstairs to grab my bag that has my bathroom items in them. I may have slept on an old pillow last night, but I'm not trusting that this place has towels. I'd much rather use my own.

The climb up and down stairs is going to take some getting used to. It is one of the reasons why I'm not a huge fan of two-story houses, normally. However, this one might be an exception. The added bonus being I don't have to pay for it. I set my bag on the bed, and pull out my towel, and everything else I need. I'll probably need to shave just in case I see my sexy rescuer again today. I'm really hoping I do. *Stop it, Stella. The promotion is all that matters. Sexy man or no sexy man.*

The bathroom is attached to the bedroom so I undress as I walk into it. The curtains are open, though I doubt anyone can see me since I have absolutely no neighbors. I reach to turn on the water but something in the tub catches my eye. "What the hell is that?" I bend down to get a closer look, and hear the hiss coming from the snake hanging out beside the drain. I shriek, grab the towel I dropped on the floor, and wrap it around me.

Is this one of those times I can call Johnny? I'm hoping like hell it is because I'm not touching that thing. I rush back into the room and grab my phone. Pressing his contact, I wait for the ringing and will him to answer. It's ringing for so long that I'm not sure he's going to answer. Just before it rolls over to voicemail, I hear his gruff voice over the line. "Hello?"

"Johnny?"

"Yeah. Stella? Is that you?"

"Yeah," I pant. "Can you come over here?"

"What's wrong?"

I don't have time to explain this to him. "I need you over as soon as possible." I'm breathing hard, and I can only imagine what I sound like to him. "Hurry, before this stupid thing tries to attack me." I hang up the phone and jump on my bed, sitting as close to the headboard as I can. There's no way I'm leaving this spot until he gets here to rescue me…once again.

All the joy and elation I felt when I walked into the house last night is gone. It went right out the window when a snake decided to slither its way up the drain into the shower. I'm not cut out for country life. Why couldn't Mr. Hart get me an apartment in town? A place that has less creepy crawlers' intent on scaring the shit out of me. I wish Johnny would hurry up and get here. I'm not prepared to deal with that thing in my bathroom. Hell, I don't know the first thing about wrangling a snake. I will just wait for Johnny to come.

I've never once needed a man to do anything for me, but I'm not too proud to admit that I'll gladly let one take care of this problem. He just needs to get his ass over here. I'm not sure why my first instinct was to call him. Maybe it was the way he helped me last night, or the fact that he told me to call him if I needed anything. I think this falls under the anything clause.

I'd be lying if I said I didn't want to see him again, though. When I fell into him last night, I felt a zing. One that I haven't felt in years. My sole focus has been on my career, and I haven't given myself time to date. The few times I've gone out, I've ended up with total assholes. It's possible my expectations are too high, and I have this weird notion that guys should be gentlemen and not obnoxious at all.

I hear footsteps pounding up the stairs to the porch, and seconds later the front door slams open. "Stella," Johnny calls. "Where are you?"

Wow, he got here faster than I thought he would. It hasn't even been a full five minutes and he's barging through my front door like some sort of superhero. "I'm upstairs," I yell to make sure he can hear me. Wait, how did he get inside. God, I'm such an idiot. I was so excited about the house last night that I didn't bother locking the door before coming upstairs. And I didn't think about it when I went downstairs earlier. *Shit*. I'm not telling

Audrey about this mishap. She'll never let me live it down and I'll get an hour-long lecture from her. I'd rather do without that, thank you very much.

I hear his boots hit every single one of the steps leading from the front door to the landing. Each thud brings him closer to getting rid of the stupid snake in my bathroom. He skids to a stop when he sees me.

Holy shit. I am not prepared for what he is wearing. Or…maybe I should say a lack of what he's wearing. A simple white T-shirt covers his broad chest, but that's not where my eyes land. Their focus is on the loose-fitting boxers covering the top half of his legs. When you add in the boots, and disheveled hair, it has every part of me buzzing with energy. These hormones need to simmer down. Now is not the time.

My gaze slowly moves up to his face, and the smirk on his face lets me know he caught me gawking. "Are you done staring?" He crosses his arms over his chest and leans against the open door. "Why did you have me rush over here? You look perfectly fine to me."

I swallow past the lump in my throat. There has never been a man that can render me speechless, and yet here I am without a word to say. A noise from the bathroom brings me back to my senses. "There's a snake in my shower." My voice comes out barely above a whisper. He makes me nervous, especially when he looks as if he just rolled out of bed.

He quirks an eyebrow and stalks toward me. "Is that who I can thank for the view this morning?" His eyes travel up and down my body. I thought I freaked him out last night, and that's why he left so abruptly. But maybe he's been thinking about me as much as I've been thinking about him. Stop, Stella. You're imagining it. It's just adrenaline from rushing over here. It doesn't mean anything. Right?

Fuck. I look down and tighten the towel wrapped around my chest. How could I forget that I don't have any clothes on? It was the last thing on my mind when the slithering thing in my shower decided to make an appearance. I swear, since meeting Johnny last night, my brain doesn't function at normal capacity anymore. I can't stop thinking about him. Hell, I even dreamed about him. It was a rather nice dream, but that's beside the point. "That's not even important." I shriek. "Can you please just get it out of my house?"

"You seemed to have forgotten about the snake long enough to ogle me." He places both hands on the foot of my bed, and leans toward me. "From where I'm standing, the snake isn't a priority."

An image of him shifting his hands higher until they wrap around my thighs, flutters through my brain, and I scoot back as if that will make it go away. The distance is a good thing. Space, that's what I need.

"Well, it's a priority for me." I am doing all I can to give off my best stuck-up and high maintenance girl vibe. Then, hopefully, he'll back off. I'm here to do my job. That's it. I don't have time to be rolling around in the sack with the locals. "Can you just go deal with it?"

"Sure," he stands up to his full height, and towers over me. I'm not short by any means, but he would still be taller than me if I wore heels. "But I want to talk to you after." He doesn't wait for me to respond. Instead, he turns his back to me and marches straight toward the bathroom. What in the world could he want to talk to me about?

A few minutes pass by, and he walks out of the bathroom with the trashcan in his hand. "Is it in there?" I'm surprised he caught it so quickly. If it were up to me, I'd burn the house down and find a new place that isn't surrounded by nature.

"Yup," he nods his head. "Do you want to see what had you so terrified?"

He tilts the trashcan toward me, and I scramble to the top of the bed. My towel is slipping, and I'm doing my best to keep it secured. "Nope. I want it out of my house. All creepy crawly things are now officially banned."

He shakes his head and laughs. "That's not how it works, City Girl."

I feel like I should be insulted by the new nickname, except it's the truth. I'm city through and through. Even though I love the house, it would be much better if it was situated in an area that had more concrete than wildlife. Without another word, he leaves my bedroom. "Where are you going?"

"To get the snake out of your house." I follow him out, and he pauses on the stairs. "Unless you want me to put him back."

"No, I'm good," I wave him off, but I'm curious now. "What are you going to do with it?"

He's already at the front door, and walking onto the porch. "I'm going to release it back into the wild."

"Why?" My voice is louder than I intended, but I don't want that thing released anywhere. "It'll just come back inside, and we'll do this all over again."

"It's a grass snake," Johnny sighs. "They aren't venomous, and they'll help take care of any rodents you have out here. Besides, I'm fine with this being a recurring event." His eyes travel from my legs to wear the towel ends just under my ass.

"Rodents," I gasp. "You mean there are mice around

here."

"Mice, possums," he shrugs. "There are things bigger, and worse, than this tiny snake out there." He points toward the woods to drive his point home. Now all I'm going to think about is four legged creatures trying to find their way into my home.

"I really didn't need that visual," I huff.

"Go take a shower, and I'll deal with the snake." He turns back toward me, "Maybe I'll even go grab something for breakfast and be back before you get out."

"And put some damn clothes on," I mutter under my breath before I walk back into my bedroom. He's entirely too distracting looking the way he does. He chuckles as he walks away from me. He wasn't supposed to hear that. One day what I think won't come out of my mouth. Today isn't that day.

Hearing the front door close, I decide to stay in the bedroom. As much as I want to follow him, if only to make sure he lets the snake loose far away from my house, it is time to jump in the shower. There's no way in hell I'm going to be known as the new girl who walks around the front yard in only a bath towel. What will the people in this tiny village think of me if word got out?

Chapter Twelve

It takes a lot of skill to wash your hair while keeping your eyes open. The only way I can ensure nothing else is going to come out of the drain is if I can see it at all times. I am not letting anything sneak up on me.

My thoughts drift to Johnny and I can't keep myself from wondering if he's back yet. I'm curious to see what he wants to talk about, and as much as I'm unwilling to have an actual relationship…I'm not opposed to a little bit of fun while I'm here. I know I said I'm here to do my job and go home, but that man is beyond delicious. Especially with this hero complex he has going on. He can save me any damn day of the week.

The sound of the squeaky bathroom door knob being turned sends heat through my body, settling between my thighs. Is Johnny walking in here? I mean, he felt comfortable enough to barge in to come to my rescue, yet again. He obviously wouldn't have any issue walking in after the way he was staring at my body earlier. He acted like a gentleman last night, but this morning, I got a glimpse of something entirely different. Today, he was much more playful, and I got the impression he is not afraid to go after what he wants. The only question is…should I make him work for it? Or, give in?

Sliding the shower curtain open, I manage to fall on my ass. My head a mere inch from smacking into the wall, and making this morning even more interesting. Tiffany and Audrey are standing on the other side of the shower giggling like they are twelve-years old. "We're here," they say in unison. Ugh, they sound like those creepy twins in the hallway from that horror movie. It's a good thing they don't look like each other, otherwise it would increase the freaky factor that much more.

"Sorry," Audrey winces. "We thought maybe you weren't in the shower yet."

"Because hearing running water wasn't a clue," I grab their outstretched hands. "Seriously, I could have busted my head open."

"But you didn't," Tiffany says with a smirk on her face.

"Do one of you assholes want to help me up?" My hands still have soap all over them and it's hard to get a grip on anything.

"By the way, who's the hunky half-dressed dude in your yard? Did you end up having a night of fun?" Tiffany asks as she give me a sly glance.

Do I really want to fill them in on this? They'll give me hell for days if I even give them the littlest bit of information about Johnny. But I guess if I do it now, I won't have to hear them nag me about it later. "Let me get this shampoo out of my hair, and I'll fill you in."

"Dude," Tiffany groans. "Why do you have so much stuff?"

Rolling my eyes, I ignore her and continue walking up the steps with the box in my hands. "I thought you were done complaining after we packed it all up."

"I was until I remembered that we have to unpack it." She pauses by the truck and looks around. "Where's Audrey?"

"Good question. I have no idea."

I set the box down inside the door, and search for my missing cousin. She's not downstairs, and I rush up to see where she's run off to. Lo and behold, she's in my room, putting my clothes into neat folded stacks on my bed. Except they aren't folded the same way I had them in the box. "What the hell are you doing?"

"Folding your clothes and putting them away. What does it look like?" She doesn't bother looking up, and moves to the next article of clothing.

"That is not folding. It looks like you're doing origami."

"I read this book about keeping everything tidy, and this is how that author folds her clothes."

I snort. "Well, I won't be folding them like that once you're gone so it's a waste of time." I snatch my pajama shorts out of her hand and toss them on the bed. "We have more boxes to unload."

"Do I have to?"

"Yep. Tiff might be complaining about it, but she didn't hide out to keep from helping." Honestly, I'm a little disappointed in Audrey. She's usually the one running full steam ahead.

"Fine," she pouts. "Let's get them all unloaded, then we can take a break."

Pfft. I shouldn't take one, but a break does sound nice. Anything to stop sweating in this stupid heat. Why can't Texas actually experience all the seasons? It would be great to feel Fall for longer than a few days. Other states get weeks, even months. Not Texas…we get Summer and Winter. There is no in-between.

Tiffany is struggling with two boxes piled on top of each other when we make it outside. "Here," I say. "Let me take one of those."

"Thanks," she breaths, and looks at Audrey. "Nice of you to join us."

"Shut up," Audrey bumps into her and the box in her hand wobbles the slightest bit.

"That better not have anything breakable in it."

Wrangling these two is going to be a pain in my ass, but at least they are here to help me. I could be doing this all alone. Although…I'm pretty sure Johnny would help me out if I needed him to. Seriously, I just met this guy. Why is he my go to person right now? Work, Stella. That is what you are here for.

We are all sitting on the front porch, bottles of water in hand when a truck rumbles down my driveway. There's only one person it can be…Johnny. I hate to admit that I've already memorized the way his truck sounds. It's an older model, but you wouldn't be able to tell with the shiny paint coating the metal. It's a deep red, almost maroon, and he looks damn fine sitting behind the wheel. I was wondering if he was actually going to come back. Luckily for him, he keeps his word. I'm starving, and I haven't had anything except coffee all day.

The truck comes to a slow stop, and he doesn't get out right away. He's staring at us as if we are insane. The second his truck door opens, the three of us stand up. Audrey is hiding behind one of the posts, and waves as he makes his way toward the porch. She's such a weirdo. I'm not sure how she even gets dates without Tiffany being the wing woman. She has no problem talking to us, but when it comes to men, it's like she loses her voice and confidence. Hopefully my time away will make her speak actual words to guys.

Before I can say hello, Tiffany speaks up. "I see you've found your clothes. What a shame," she shakes her head. Leave it to her to say exactly what she's thinking.

"Funny thing," he shrugs. "They were in my closet this whole time. Who knew?" His steps are long and measured as he walks up the porch stairs. He has a purpose for being here, and I'm terrified of what it might be. "Can I speak with you, Stella?" He waves the box of what I can now see are donuts as a bribe.

My eyes widen, and I nod. Deer meet headlights. What can I say, I'm a total sucker for a man with donuts. "Yeah, sure." I walk toward the open front door, but pause and wave my hand at my cousins. I'm horrible for not introducing the minute he got out of the truck. "I'd like you to meet my cousins, Audrey and Tiffany. This is Johnny."

I don't say anything else, or wait for them to respond. I don't miss one of them whispering, "Oh, they're going inside to talk." It has to be Tiffany because she snorts then laughs obnoxiously. She's also the only one who would even say something like that within hearing distance. I'm going to strangle her.

I walk into the kitchen and lean against the counter opposite of the island. Johnny sets the box down, and I'm grateful that he came back at all. The food is just icing on the cake. I cross my arms against my chest, hoping like hell it doesn't show all of my cleavage. Not that it matters after he saw almost my entire body this morning. "Ignore them, they are beyond ridiculous." My eyes search out anything but him.

"Eh, they're just having fun." I watch him study the kitchen out of the corner of my eye. He looks impressed, and I wonder what it looked like before I moved in. When his eyes meet mine, his breath hitches. He shoves his hands in his pockets and stands straighter. "Besides, I was half naked when they saw me for the first time. I'm pretty sure their thoughts went down the gutter right then and there."

"I've assured them that nothing happened between us, and that you were only here because of a stupid snake. They really need to learn to mind their own business instead of trying to get into mine." I reach for a donut, but he slides the box away.

He rushes around the island until he's standing directly in front of me. He's too close, and he smells really good. Nothing like the men in the city. It's woodsy, as if he spends a lot of time outdoors. "That can wait." I open my mouth to protest. Except he places a finger against my mouth, effectively cutting me off. Jerking my head back, I stare at him. He actually touched me. "I have a feeling you wouldn't have been too upset if something more did happen."

My cheeks burn, and I'm pretty sure I've given away what I was thinking. "You," I stutter. "You have no way of knowing that." I try to back away, but the stupid counter is behind me and I have nowhere to go.

He places his hands on the counter, boxing me in. Too

close. Way too close. I can't think when he's right here, in my space. "Tell me that you aren't attracted to me in any way, and I will lay off. I'll talk to you about your car, and we can act as if we've never seen each other half naked." When I don't respond, he continues. "Or, I can talk to you about your car and we can have a little fun while you're here."

"What do you mean by fun?" My voice is husky, giving him the answer he wants.

"You know exactly what I mean." He leans closer, his lips a breath away from my ear. "No strings attached. You, me, and whatever we can think of to fill the time. Something to ease the stress of you missing home."

I duck under his arms, grab a donut, and back away from him. "That's pretty forward considering I don't even know you." I take a bite and continue walking backward until I run into the refrigerator. *Damn it*. I really need to learn the layout of this kitchen.

"That's the beauty of it," he says. "We're practically strangers. How long are you staying in town?" That probably would have been the better question for him to lead with. Not that I'm going to say yes, or anything.

"Two or three months, I think," I say around a mouthful of donut. Maybe that will be enough to ward him away.

"See," he argues, as if I've just cleared everything up. "That's not long enough for us to develop real feelings for each other. Hell, we don't even have to be exclusive with each other if it makes you feel better." He must see the disgusted look on my face because he corrects himself. "Or, we can. It's up to you." This man has lost his damn mind if he thinks I'm just going to jump into bed with him. It also makes me wonder what's wrong with him that he doesn't have a girlfriend already. "We don't have to see each other regularly. Whatever you decide is what will happen."

He sounds desperate now, and my defenses are up. "I'll have to think about it." I can't believe I'm actually considering this. "Until I decide, are you good with being friends seeing as you're the only person I know in this town."

"Sure." He smiles. Ugh, that smile is enough to make my panties drop straight to the floor. "If you change your mind, just let me know." He winks at me.

I move toward the box of donuts again, picking one up. "Now that whatever that was is out of the way, what did you want to discuss about my car?"

Chapter Thirteen

"So, are you going to take him up on his offer?" Tiffany and I are sitting at the kitchen table waiting for Audrey to return with the pizza. She didn't trust Tiffany to drive the rental truck to get food since it's in her name.

"I don't know," I bury my face in my hands. "I don't even know him. Besides, before we have any of these discussions, shouldn't we wait until Audrey gets back?"

Tiffany snorts. "Hell no. She is the voice of reason, and you listen to her way too much anyway." She pulls my hands from my face. "This is the perfect situation. He's not looking for anyone permanent, and neither are you. You can get your job done, and have a little fun on the side."

"But what if I catch feelings? Or my sexcapades with him interfere with my job? I can't afford for this project to go down in flames. I need this job." I scoot my chair back and stand up. "This could go wrong on so many levels." It's a good thing I'm wearing flipflops. Otherwise, my feet would be aching in the heels I typically wear with all the pacing I'm doing.

Now, it's Tiffany's turn to stand up. She rounds the

table and grabs my shoulders. She's the baby out of the three of us, and almost four years younger than me. Taking her advice would be a lot easier if she had her shit in order and didn't move wherever the wind blows her. "Stop worrying so much. You have an amazing job that you've busted your ass for, and this distribution center is going to be up and running without a hitch. Go out and have fun. It's a win, win situation."

"Spoken like somebody who doesn't have any responsibilities," I sigh. She jerks her hands away from me, and hurt flashes across her face. "Sorry, I didn't mean it like that. I just don't know how to be like you."

She forces a smile onto her face and shrugs. "No biggie." She's playing it off, but I know my words hurt her more than she's willing to let on. "Just try not to overthink things. It's how I get through life; you don't see me stressing out over every little thing."

I'm choosing to let that last jab go because what I said was kind of bitchy. Maybe I should take her advice, though. Let loose and enjoy myself while I'm here.

"Dammit," Audrey's voice comes from the front of the house. "I am really missing the city right now. We could've had our food delivered to us within fifteen minutes. I wouldn't be struggling to open a door and carry three pizza boxes into a house I'm not familiar with." She grunts, and I hear a box slide. "A little help here would be nice."

Oh shit, Audrey is about to get pissed. She looks sweet and innocent, but when she loses her temper, it's not pretty. Instead of fighting over who is going to help her, we both run to the front door. Neither of us wants to frustrate her more than she already is. "Let me have those," I say grabbing the boxes out of her hands. "Thanks," she slips her shoes off before heading for the kitchen. "Tiff, can you go grab the wine out of the truck?"

"Sure thing," Tiffany salutes her. I can see why she decided to talk to me before Audrey came back. She didn't want me to get a "mom" lecture.

Audrey is pulling plates out of a box as I set the pizzas down. "You realize this place isn't even a town, right? Asheville reminds me of where you lived when we were kids. This…this is a village."

"I know," I groan. "It's not exactly what I was expecting, but I can't complain too much. I mean, it is free since the company is paying for it."

"Which is good," she agrees. "I just think living here is going to be hard for you without all the hustle and bustle of the city. You wanted to escape this life growing up, and you ended up in the small-town life again. Even if it's only for a short period of time."

"Who knows," I shrug. "It may not be all that bad."

"Please tell me you aren't considering getting involved with that guy," Audrey sighs.

Tiffany walks in with two bottles of wine, and stops in her tracks. Instead of putting in her two cents because it will get her nowhere with Audrey, she sets the bottles on the counter and begins searching for the wine glasses I packed. "I have a feeling we're going to need this," she whispers as she passes by me.

"Is it such a bad thing if I do?" I ask. "It's not like I'm staying here."

"He's a distraction, Stella," she stares at me, waiting for me to back down. For someone without kids, she sure does know how to use the scary mom voice. "You were the first one to tell us that your focus has to be your job. It's all about our promotion, remember?"

I roll my eyes. She's way too damn young to be giving me this speech. I've done nothing but focus on my career. I've pushed aside dates, and sacrificed having a life so I could work my way up the corporate ladder. Is it such a bad thing to veer off the path? "Let's not talk about it anymore tonight. Y'all are leaving in the morning, and we should make the most of tonight." Tiffany shoves a glass of wine in my hand before pouring one for her and Audrey. "I won't be in the same city as y'all for a few months."

"Lucky," Tiffany mumbles under her breath. It takes everything in me to hold back my laugh. This is exactly the type of escape she would welcome.

"Fine," Audrey agrees. "Here's to getting the distribution center up and running, and a future promotion."

As much as these two drive me crazy, I'm going to miss seeing them on a regular basis. Even though we can video each other, it's just not the same. They won't be here to tell me when to cover my eyes in scary movies, or drink with me when the job is getting to be too much. We clink our glasses together, and take a drink. I think they feel the same way.

Last night I didn't sleep well once Audrey and Tiffany left. I felt completely alone. Everything here is so quiet. There's no traffic noise, or sirens, to fill the background. All I can hear is the water hitting the bottom of the shower or the wind rustling leaves outside my window. I plan on downloading one of those white noise apps on my phone to make me feel more at home when I go to bed tonight.

One thing is for sure, I will not be watching any horror

movies while I'm here. This entire scenario is how they all start out. A girl alone in a house surrounded by a wooded area. No thank you, I choose life.

I sigh, as I pull out my clothes for my first day of work. I don't know anyone here, and I'm not sure how I'll be received. Small towns are known for being leery of outsiders, or at least in my experience. It's okay if I don't become chummy with the people here. It's not like I'll be here forever. Two months and I'm gone, back to the city where I belong.

My shower is quick. My eyes stay trained on bottom of the tub thanks to my new fear of snakes from a drain. Mondays are already hard enough. I don't need to be freaked out about one more thing. Of course, I could call Johnny to rescue me, but he's already supposed to be arranging something for me to get to work. I think he mentioned taking me in himself, if need be, until I can get a rental car. Being a burden to him isn't something I want to do, though. He has to have his own things he needs to get done. Chauffeuring me around shouldn't be one of them.

I almost slip on the tile floor as I get out of the shower. The box full of bathroom stuff is one of the few I haven't unpacked yet. I'm kicking myself for not doing that last night. This floor is slippery with condensation after my shower and I'm not a fan. My house in Austin would probably be the same way without my lush rug right in front of the shower entrance.

Getting dressed doesn't take me long, thanks to setting out my clothes beforehand. It always pays to be prepared, at least in this instance. Nerves creep along my spine, and I wish they would stop. This isn't something that's ever happened to me. Not even when I interviewed in front of Mr. Hart for the first time all those years ago.

This feels different, somehow. For the company, so much hinges on this center being up and running as fast as possible, and for me, I can't even think about how everything going smoothly could affect my position in the company. Success is the only option I have.

Up or down? That's the question that keeps running through my brain as I'm fixing my hair. I feel like down would make me seem more laid-back, but up will make me look professional. It's hard enough being a woman in management, and I don't want a new group of people to make any assumptions about me. I remember how judgmental some small-town communities can be. It seems so inconsequential to worry about how my hairstyle makes me look, but they need to know that I should be taken seriously.

In the end I decide to split it. My blonde hair is resting against my back, but the front is pulled back and held firmly in place with a barrette. Fingers crossed I made my first correct decision for the day.

The smell of coffee fills the house, and I inhale deeply. I will forever love Audrey for getting me a coffee pot, with a timer, for my birthday. I don't have to waste time in the mornings, going through the motions. All I have to do is add my cream and sugar, and I'm ready to go. It's the perfect solution to getting my ass in gear in the mornings. And if I oversleep, which has been known to happen, it will wake me up.

With my travel mug of caffeinated heaven, I step out onto the front porch looking for Johnny. He isn't here, but there is a car in my driveway. One I don't recognize. *What the hell?* Who would leave a car that obviously isn't mine in the driveway? A part of me is leery of walking toward it, but there is a square piece of paper tucked underneath the windshield wiper, and my curiosity gets the best of me as usual.

The handwriting is almost illegible. But I see Johnny's name at the bottom, and any uncertainty I had melts away.

Stella,

I had to go into work early this morning so I could order a few things for your car. This is my mom's old car, and she said it was okay for you to use it. Everything works great and it will get you where you need to go until you get a rental, or I get your car fixed.

Johnny

Wow, his mom must be very trusting. There's no way in hell I would let someone I don't know borrow my car. I don't even let Tiffany use my car, and she's my cousin. I'm tempted to leave it parked in my driveway and call an Uber to come pick me up, except I'm running late and I doubt they have that type of service out in the boonies. Reason number five hundred and sixty-five why I miss the city.

Chapter Fourteen

THE MAPS APP on my phone directs me to the distribution center. It doesn't take nearly as long as I thought it would, and it's only a few miles outside of Asheville. I hope Asheville has a decent bar so I can go to at the end of the day to unwind. The only thing that would make it better is if it was within walking distance from my place so I wouldn't have to drive like it is back at home.

Looking around the site where the new distribution center will be, the only person I come into contact with on my way into the building is one of the construction workers. "Can you tell me where the foreman is?"

"Sure thing," he sets down the tool bag he's carrying in his hand. "If you go through those doors," he points to the double metal doors in front of us. "And take a right, he should be putting the last touches on the office."

"Thanks." It's odd that he didn't even ask who I was. If a stranger walked onto a jobsite in a city, there's no doubt in my mind they would be asking who they were and what their business was. Way too damn trusting. Though that may work in my favor when I start hiring people. Unless of course, they are leery of "outsiders."

I am not sure if it is the tapping of my heels on the new floor or the sound of my heart thudding in my chest, but they are drowning out the sound of power tools all around me. My pesky nerves are back, and I need to dispel them before I meet with the foreman.

To my right is the office. The flickering fluorescent light giving the space a creepy feeling. I'm not looking forward to spending most of my time in there. Maybe I can bring a lamp in to keep the office illuminated and not have to turn those lights on.

"Can I help you?" A man with broad shoulders asks as I step inside. He doesn't look amused that a stranger is walking into his domain.

"Actually, you can," I nod my head and hold my hand out to shake his. "I'm Stella. Mr. Hart said you would be expecting me."

"Oh," he gives my hand a quick shake. "I'm Chance, and the foreman of this operation. I was just finishing up the desk. I can be out of your way in the next fifteen minutes."

"Thank you," I reply. "How much longer do you think it will take to finish the building?" Normally I would lead into this question with small talk, but I also have a Job Fair to plan, and I need to know when I can do that. The sooner I can get employees here and running things, the sooner I can go home.

He shrugs his shoulders, "Maybe a week. We didn't have any other jobs vying for our attention, so we were able to complete this faster than anticipated. Right now, we're a month ahead of schedule."

"That's great," I exclaim. "It will work out perfectly with the rest of my plans."

"Glad we could help," he says. "I'm all done here. If you need anything, just holler. Myself or one of my guys will be able to help."

Left alone in the room, I can hear the sounds of drills down the hall. I have the distinct impression that these are going to be make up the soundtrack to next week as they finish up the building. Right now, there isn't much to work with, but that's okay. I can at least start getting everything organized. This way, it will all be ready to go when I hand this job over to whoever we hire. Hopefully, Mr. Hart has someone in mind, or else I'll have to start from scratch.

Taking a small break, I send Johnny a text.

Stella: Thanks for letting me borrow your mom's car. Is there anything she really likes I can give her to show my gratitude? Also, what's your address?

I wait a few moments for him to respond, but he doesn't. He must be busy at work. I'll probably grab a gift card of some sort, or wine, on my way home to give Johnny's mom. Hopefully, he'll give me his address and will be home when I decide to leave for the day. I need to see him, and consider this "friends with benefits" situation.

Looking at my phone one more time, I decide to stop waiting for a response and get my butt back in gear. I can do this. First, I will make this office a welcoming space for the new manager. After that, I can start planning the Job Fair.

Gone Country

Damn it, I should have paid more attention to where Johnny lived when he brought my car here the other night. He never replied to my message, and I feel like a dumbass for sending it. All I know is it's off the main road that cuts through town.

I slow down at every driveway entrance, searching for signs of my car. It's the only clue I have to finding his house. Fear of passing it sears through me. I'm getting closer to my house, and I still haven't spotted any possible candidates for his place. Maybe I should give up and go home. He'll text me when he gets the chance. I'm almost to the turnoff for my house when I spot my car outside a barn. That kind of matches the description Johnny gave of where he was leaving my car. Whipping into the driveway, I throw my hand in the air. Victory is mine. Holy shit, I can't believe I actually found it.

The butterflies in my stomach die at the realization as I notice his truck is nowhere in sight. I guess he's still at work. I can at least leave the gift I bought for his mom. No use wasting the trip, even if it is practically around the corner from me. I grab the bottle off the passenger seat, and search through the console for a scrap of paper. All I see is a couple of bank pens and some fast food napkins. That will have to work.

You weren't home when I stopped by. If you look to your right, there's a bottle of wine for your mom. I didn't know what to get her, but I wanted to do something to tell her thank you for letting me borrow her car. Hope she likes red. Can you take it to her for me? Also, call me so I know you got this.

Thanks,
Stella

My fingers are crossed that the wine doesn't get too hot before he gets home. Then I'll have to go buy something else. Not that it's a problem, but I don't know the woman, and I'm not certain she'll even like the wine.

Despite my claim of wanting to only be friends, the ball is now in his court. It's his turn to reach out to me. I'll know he's serious if he does. If he doesn't…I'm glad I didn't waste my time.

I hurry back to the car, escaping the heat the only other thing on my mind besides Johnny. There are still a few boxes of decorations I need to unpack. They are the last things that will make the house feel like it's truly my space for the duration of my stay.

My phone rings and I almost fall off the sofa. Ugh, this thing is not as comfortable as it looks. I wish they would have updated the furniture in here when they remodeled the rest of the house. I grab the ringing phone from the coffee table, and answer it before it goes to voicemail. "Hello." Good Lord is my voice really as deep as it sounds.

"Did I wake you?" I blink in confusion for a bit, then pull the screen back to see who's calling…Johnny.

I should have known it was him as soon as I answered. It's not like there are a ton of guys that call me at any given moment. "Damn. I must have dozed off," I sigh. "Did you get the bottle of wine I left for your mom?"

I take a second to wonder why he's calling before I remember that I asked him to. "Yep," he says. "I'll make sure to get it to her." Silence fills the receiver, and it's becoming awkward. "You should probably go back to sleep."

"It's okay. I need to stay awake." My mouth opens wide as I yawn. "Was there something else you needed?"

He doesn't miss a beat. "I was giving you a call per your note. But I also wanted to see if you've eaten yet."

My stomach growls, answering the question, but it's probably quiet enough that he doesn't hear it. "Actually, no." I stand up, needing to get off the couch before I'm stuck, or fall back to sleep.

"Do you want to come over for a late dinner?"

Should I or shouldn't I? I did say that it's his move, and he just made it. "Sure. What time do you want me there?"

"Anytime." His voice hitches, and it's adorable that I make him nervous. Especially after he came to my house and went all Alpha male on me. It only makes me want to figure him out even more.

"Okay, I'll be there in twenty." It's a good thing I know where he lives now. Downside, I have no clue what the hell I'm supposed to wear. Do I wear the leggings and t-shirt I have on now? Or, do I put something else? So many decisions.

"Sounds good. I'll see you then."

"Bye," I say and hang up before he can say anything else. Are we hanging out as friends, or is this a date? I mean friends hang out and eat dinner together. I need to see what other options I have for clothes. What I am wearing doesn't feel like it's right. It definitely sends the "friend zone" message loud and clear, but just because he's there now doesn't mean I want him to stay in that compartment until I leave.

Chapter Fifteen

Geez, he lives less than five minutes from my house, and I've still somehow managed to show up later than planned. In my defense, I had to make sure my makeup was on point without looking like I'm trying too hard. I don't know why I am trying to impress a man I barely know. I need to be focusing my attention, making sure this center opens with a bang, not on how handsome this man is. Yet, here I am, at his house for dinner.

The front door swings open before my foot touches the porch. "You scared the hell out of me."

"Sorry," he shrinks back. "I didn't want you to trip over anything since I haven't replaced the light out here, yet." He opens the door wider, inviting me in.

"Any chance you've fixed the floor in the kitchen. I don't want to fall through it again." I search for a wall peg to hold my bag to no avail. Instead, I set it on the small entryway table.

"Not yet," he shrugs. "It will have to wait until I have some free time since *someone*," he points his finger at me, "derailed my plans the other night. Besides, you wouldn't have fallen through it if you weren't being nosy."

"That wasn't my fault! I can't control things that run out in front of moving objects," I huff.

"I was just giving you a hard time." Johnny's shoulders shake with laughter he's trying to hide. "I'm glad you don't deny being nosy, though."

"Eh," I shrug my shoulders. "I needed to know what kind of person you were. And…to make sure you weren't a serial killer."

"You probably should have thought about that before you willingly got in my truck. What would you have done if I had no intention of bringing you to my house? Or actually helping you?"

"I guess it's a good thing we don't have to worry about that since you aren't *actually* dangerous. Besides, I'm sure I would have come up with something if my life was on the line." I wave his concern away, but he is eyeing me as if he wants to devour me whole. I've never been a huge fan of fairy tales, but I'd play the little red riding hood to his big bad wolf. He's obviously not as gentlemanly as I assumed. "Didn't you say you were cooking for me?" Talk about an abrupt subject change. Could I have made it anymore noticeable?

He laughs, walking around me and toward the oven. "You're lucky I didn't already eat. I thought you might stand me up when you didn't show up when you said you would." He's pulling pans out of the oven and sets them on the counter in front of him.

"There is no way I'd be a no show when food is involved. I very rarely get home-cooked meals." I watch his arms flex with every movement as he preps our plates. "I am sorry for getting here late. I had to figure out where

Audrey put all the clothes she unpacked." Not entirely a lie.

"You must be busy if you never get a home cooked meal."

"I'm practically married to my job. No rest for the wicked and all that. My cousins wouldn't mind me taking more time off, though."

"Y'all seem pretty close." He adds macaroni and green beans to the pork chops on the plates.

"Yep. They are my best friends. We've been close since we were kids. Spent summers together, and called each other all the time. Our parents weren't fans of the phone bills, but I think they're happy we stayed in touch. When they graduated from high school, they left home and moved to Austin near me."

"Wow. I can't imagine moving across the state for anyone in my family." He grabs some silverware and motions me to follow him. "I hope it's okay with you if we eat in the living room seeing as how I don't have a kitchen table."

"That's fine with me." I take a seat on the sofa while he sets the plates on the coffee table. "I only eat at my table when Audrey and Tiffany come over. There's no sense going through the whole routine when it's only me."

"We might be more alike than you think. Let me grab us some drinks. Anything in particular that you want?"

"I'm good with water, thank you." Johnny turns toward the kitchen, and I'd be a liar if I said I wasn't checking out his ass. "Do you have any siblings?"

"Yeah," he hollers from the kitchen. "I have three brothers. After graduating, they left as soon as they could." He comes back and hands me one of two bottles of water. "They wanted to look for something bigger and better. I guess they seemed to have found it. I only see them a few times a year around the holidays."

"I can't imagine only seeing people I grew up with a handful of times a year. Hell, I'm not certain how I'm going to handle not seeing Audrey and Tiff every few days."

"I do believe I offered a way to distract you," he winks at me, and grabs his knife and fork. "Dig in before it's too cold to taste good."

I do as he says and moan as I bite into the pork chop. It's grilled with a hint of Italian seasoning. Anytime I've had chops on the grill they are sticky with barbecue sauce. These are perfection and I bypass using my fork and knife. Holding the meat between my fingers, I take another bite. It may not be ladylike, but he doesn't seem to mind.

"You need to stop making noises like that, or you're going to give me the wrong impression."

Maybe I want to give him that impression, even if I'm not doing it intentionally. This food is just *that* good. "I've never had chops cooked like this before. They're delicious."

"Stick around long enough and I'll show you how to make them. It's not hard."

His offer to be whatever I want flits through my mind. Would it be so bad to have a little fun while I'm here? Audrey is definitely not in my corner on this, but Tiffany has my back. What would it hurt? It's not like I'll be here long enough to catch feelings or anything. Having someone to do things with is totally reasonable, and if we end up in his bed, or mine, so be it.

∼

The rest of the night goes by in a blur. He now knows all the horrible pranks my cousins and I played on each other as children, including the time Tiffany tried to make Audrey eat a dead frog. That didn't go over well with any of our parents. The shitty part was I got blamed for it. I'm the oldest and was supposed to set an example. Not let them act like the kids in *Lord of the Flies*.

I glance at the clock hanging above his television. Holy shit, it's midnight. I need to get home if I'm going to get enough sleep for work tomorrow. There's so much I need to do to prepare for the Job Fair.

"Why do I get the impression you're about to rush out the front door?" Johnny's voice breaks into my thoughts.

"Because I have to get to bed. I'm not a morning person, and I have so much to do tomorrow." I don't want to leave, but even if I'm planning on taking him up on his no strings offer, I don't put out on the first date. If that's what this is.

"You could always stay," he suggests.

"As tempting as the offer is, I really need to go. It's not like I live far away." If I did, my ass wouldn't be going anywhere. It would be the perfect excuse, but alas I'm minutes down the road.

"Okay, let me walk you to your car." He grabs my hand, and pulls me off the sofa. "You never know what wild animals lurk in the woods."

"Thank you for that frightening thought because living in the middle of nowhere by myself, isn't creepy enough." I pull the car key from my pocket, and notice that he still hasn't released my hand. I'm not going to say anything because it feels nice. Not only did this man cook for me, but he's the type of person to make sure I get to my car safely. Well, his mom's car.

He doesn't bother closing the front door as he leads me outside down the steps. I hope mosquitos don't invade his house. The ones I've seen could almost pass as small birds. He hesitates after opening the car door for me. "I had fun tonight."

"Me, too." It's shocking how easy it was to talk to him. All the past blind dates I've gone on have been dull, and quiet. Nothing like tonight. "Maybe next time I can cook you dinner."

"Sounds like a plan." He lets go of my hand, and takes a step backward. "Be careful on your way home."

The urge to kiss him is overwhelming. I may not jump in bed with someone on the first date, but I'm not opposed to kissing. I stand on my tiptoes, and press a quick peck on his lips. I begin sliding into the driver seat, but I don't make it far. Johnny pulls me toward him, wraps one arm around my waist, and uses his free hand to cup the back of my neck. His lips crash into mine, and I feel the electricity down to my toes. He kisses me like a man possessed, and I'm his way to freedom.

I pull back, unable to form words. He, on the other hand, grins. "Text me when you get home."

He doesn't say anything else. Just walks back to his porch and waits for me to get in the car. He doesn't go inside until I put the car in reverse. This man will be the death of any self-restraint I thought I had.

Chapter Sixteen

SHIT. Where the hell, did I leave my purse? I scour the car to see if maybe it slipped under one of the seats, and have zero luck. Running back up the porch stairs, I check the kitchen, the cabinets, and the refrigerator. The refrigerator thing is because of my aunts. Anytime they take a dish to whatever event they are attending they put their keys in the refrigerator so they don't forget their dishes. It's weird, and I have no clue why I would shove my purse in there, but it's worth a look. Too bad it's not in there.

I keep replaying my drive home last night. Did I even have it? I remember taking it inside Johnny's house and setting it on the table. *Damn it*. I never grabbed it on the way out. My mind was too focused on my hand in his, and then the kiss. Thank God I keep my phone in my pocket. Otherwise, I would have forgotten that, too. I grab it off the kitchen table and press Johnny's name.

Come on, come on, pick up the phone. "Hello?" His voice is gruff, and I can hear metal hitting metal in the background.

"Um, are you at work?" I feel horrible for bugging him

if he is. That's totally unprofessional, and he seems to be extremely dedicated to his job. Almost as much as I am.

"Yeah, is something wrong?"

"Actually, yeah. Did I happen to leave my purse at your place last night?" Please say yes.

He laughs. This really isn't a laughing matter, but I guess I'm happy he's finding some humor in it. "Go check by your back door. I hid it behind the bush on the right side. I figured you might need it."

"You are a lifesaver. Thank you so much." I rush to the back door, and see the bush he mentioned. "Wait, nothing is going to attack me, right?"

"Grab a stick and wave it around in there first if you're scared."

"Are you mocking me?"

"Not at all." If it was possible to hear a smile, that's what it sounds like right now. "I just know you don't do country life."

Against my better judgement I stick my hand in the space between the wall and greenery. A sigh escapes me when my fingers brush the fabric of my purse. "Got it. I don't know how I would have gotten through today without this. I have to get things rolling for the Job Fair in a couple of weeks."

"No problem." He's quiet for a moment, and I hear someone call his name.

"You're busy. I'll talk to you later."

"Wait. What are you doing when you get off work?"

I walk back inside then my city girl instincts kick in as I close and lock the door behind me. There may not be any neighbors, but I'm not about to leave anyone easy access to get it. "Nothing. It's not like I know anyone here."

"Let's change that," he says. "Meet me after you get off and we can grab a drink."

Should I or shouldn't I? How are we supposed to keep it casual if we see each other on a daily basis?

He has to know I'm hesitating. "No pressure. We can go out as *friends*."

I don't miss the way he says friends. There's no way we can be just friends. Not after that kiss last night and how he set every part of me on fire. Screw it. If I'm going to do this, I might as well go all in. "Just give me the name and time. I'll be there."

"Great," he breathes. "I'll text you during my lunch break. See you later." Then he hangs up. He really needs to learn how to say "bye" or something. It annoys the hell out of me.

With my phone, and now my purse, in hand, it's time for this lady to get to work and kick some ass. It may only be my second day at the center, but I can already taste that promotion.

As I make preparations for the Job Fair I'll be holding, I am relieved that the all vendors accept email inquiries. If not…I'd be screwed. Well, not completely. I'd just have to make the calls from home and I don't want to do that here. The goal while I'm working in Asheville is to leave work at work. It's a lot easier since I don't have Mr. Granger's constant requests to bog me down. Maybe I'll even make some new friends with all this extra time I have. Or… maybe I'll spend a lot of time with Johnny. Right now, it could go either way.

I am anxious to meet him tonight. It's one thing to have

Gone Country

dinner with him at his house, and quite another to be out in public with him. What if he leaves me alone at the bar? Being a shy wallflower is more Audrey's area of expertise, but I don't know *anyone* here. I'm terrified that the locals won't like me. This is why I love the city. Even if I make an ass of myself, the likelihood that I'll see any of those people again is slim. Here, though, I can tell it's a place where everyone knows everything.

Ugh, why did I decide this was a good idea? Next time Tiffany tells me I should go with the flow on something, I'm going to kick her in the ass. I'm not as uptight as Audrey, but I'm also nowhere near free spirited as Tiff. One day I'll learn my lesson, but today is not that day.

My phone rings, and I jump. My knee hits the underside of the desk, and pain shoots through my leg. Grabbing my phone, I check the screen to see who's calling. Damn, it's Mr. Hart. It's kind of odd that he's calling so soon after my arrival, but maybe not. Either way, I have to answer it.

"Hello." I pitch my voice an octave higher, and throw all the confidence I can muster into the greeting.

"Hello, Stella. How is everything going in Asheville?"

"Great," I squeak. He rivals Johnny when it comes to making me nervous, but in completely different ways. This man holds my future at the company in the palm of his hands. Johnny, on the other hand...well, I'm not entirely sure what he holds. I only know that he makes me want things I haven't wanted in a *very* long time.

"That's good." I imagine him nodding and tapping his fingers on his desk. It's something I've noticed him do during meetings. "Do you think we'll be able to open on the scheduled date?"

"If the construction crew keeps going at the rate they

are right now, we may be able to open early." I clear my throat to tamp down my excitement at how easy this is going to be. "Unless, of course, you want to keep the original date."

"We will see how the Job Fair goes. Do you have any ideas on that, yet?"

"Yes, Sir. I'm working on that right now." I click my pen, anxious to get off the phone and back to work. "As soon as I finish emailing vendors about table and chair rentals, I'm going to check in and see what we need to stock the warehouse with before opening."

"Sounds good," he says. "Email me an update at the end of the week, please."

"I will. Have a great day Mr. Hart."

"You, too. Goodbye."

I tell him bye and hang up the phone. At least the big boss has manners, unlike some people I know. My phone dings with a text message. Speak of the devil.

Johnny: Meet me at Out of the Ashes at 6.
Stella: Someone is a bit demanding.
Johnny: You already agreed to go. :P I'm just giving you a place and time.
Stella: I guess. You could have said please.
Johnny: That's a no. If I formed it as a question, that gives you an opportunity to back out of our date.
Stella: Date? I thought we were going as "friends."
Johnny: I mean, if you want to look at it that way, and keep lying to yourself, that's your prerogative.
Stella: Fine. You might have a point. I'll see you there. Just know that I'll be hungry so they better have food.
Johnny: They have the best wings in town.

If I keep replying, I'll never get any work done. Putting my phone on airplane mode, I get back in gear. There's a lot to do, and while I have a couple of months to complete it, I'd rather not be scrambling at the last minute. That would only prove that I'm not ready to move up in the company, and Mr. Granger would be right. There's no way in hell I'm allowing that to happen.

Chapter Seventeen

OUT OF THE Ashes is not at all what I was expecting. If a bar in Austin had a name like that, it would be a swanky hot spot. The place I've just pulled into looks like a dive bar with bathrooms that probably haven't been cleaned in ages. I know it's wrong of me to make that assumption, but for fucks sake. The paint on the sign is wearing off, and half the letters of the flashing "Open" sign are dull and barely visible.

Now would be the time to back out of this parking space and head home. There's a bottle of wine, and a frozen pizza, waiting for me. A totally balanced meal for a single woman.

Unfortunately, a shadow blocks the dying sunlight in front of my window. There's a knock on the glass, and Johnny peers down at me. I roll down the window and stare up at him, mouth gaping. He's in what I'm assuming is his work uniform, and I thought he looked hot as hell before. The stray grease marks and disheveled hair has me squeezing my legs together. "You weren't about to bail on me, were you?"

"Pfft," I snort. "No, why would you think that? Besides, how did you know this was the car I was in?"

"You had the car in reverse," he grins, knowing damn well he caught me in a lie. "And don't forget, you're in my mom's car. I spent enough time hiding from it when I was in my teens to know whose car it is."

I guess he has a point. And I'm the dumbass that totally forgot that I am, in fact, in his mom's car. "When do you think my car will be ready?"

"We can talk about that inside." He opens the door, and holds his hand out to me. I sigh, and turn the car off. "I promise it's not as sketchy as it looks." He nods toward the building in question. "I've been coming here for as long as I remember. I wouldn't take you somewhere shady for our first official date."

I roll my eyes at his use of the word *date*. "If you say so. But, if it sucks and I don't like it, you owe me a bottle of wine." Who the hell is this flirty version of me, and where did she come from? I don't know why, but Johnny, the guy I have known for *less* than a week, makes this girl come out.

"Deal." He holds my hand all the way to the entrance, only releasing it to hold the door open for me, and a few other people who are walking out. He's the best of both worlds from what I can tell—a gentleman in public and demanding in private. I believe this is something I can work with. As long as the stupid butterflies flitting around my stomach calm their shit. There are no emotions allowed. This is temporary. *Just keep telling yourself that.*

Looks can definitely be deceiving. From the outside this bar appears shady as hell. The inside though…it's as modern and sleek as the places I frequent in Austin.

"I take it you're surprised." A soft chuckle brushes

against my neck. He wraps his arm around my waist and leads me toward a table by one of the few windows. "I told you I would never take you to a shithole on a date."

"So, you would take me to one if we weren't on one?" His raised eyebrow tells me I screwed up. "I mean," I stutter. "Not that this is a *date*. I still haven't completely agreed to anything."

"But you're considering it, and that's all that matters."

The smug grin on his face makes me want to smack him and kiss him. All of these contradicting emotions are driving me crazy. Johnny is so unlike the few men I've dated. He's just as over-confident, but he has a gentleness I've never experienced before. At least, not since my high school puppy love days. Ugh, stupid feelings need to go away. I don't have time for this.

"Stella," Johnny's voice interrupts my thoughts.

"Huh." He's staring at me and a waitress is standing at the edge of our booth. She is stunning. One of those women that will make everyone look twice with long curled blonde hair, sun-kissed skin, and shorts that are so short it's a wonder you can't see everything. There's no way in hell I'd ever be confident enough to wear anything like that unless I'm in the comfort of my own home. Maybe not even then.

"What do you want to drink?" He waves his hand toward the woman.

"Oh, sorry." My cheeks warm, and I wonder how long she's been there. Hopefully not long, or that would be embarrassing. "Whiskey sour, please."

"No problem." She taps the table, "I'll get those right out for you."

"Thanks, Angie." To his credit, he doesn't watch her walk away. That's surprising. Most guys at least glance at a beautiful woman. All the guys I dated would have, anyway. Proof that I have horrible taste in men, and maybe this isn't a good idea.

"A penny for your thoughts." He leans forward, forearms resting on the table. He's nuts if he thinks I'm going to tell him what's on my mind.

"Nothing. My mind just wandered off for a second." I pick up the menu Angie set down in front of me. "So, what's good to eat here?"

Johnny smirks and sits up, picking up his own menu. "Everything. I haven't had a bad dish in all the years I've been coming."

"Well, that narrows it down," I laugh. "What's with this place anyway? The outside looks like a decrepit building."

He shrugs and puts his menu down. I don't think he even looked at it. He was humoring me. "It's old."

"I don't mean anything bad by that. It's only that the inside and outside don't match at all. They could get some serious business if they updated and spruced it up. That's the first thing customers see, and likely turns them away."

"Everyone who lives in Asheville knows where it is. But, according to Angie, it's on her list of things to do."

"She owns this bar?" That makes me sound bitchy, but I fully expected some older man to own it.

"Yep," he crosses his arms over his chest, and his muscles bulge in the tight sleeves. I guess working on cars has some added benefits. "She inherited it from her father when he passed away. When he owned it, it was just another bar where the local drunks hung out. Then Angie took over and gutted the inside updating everything in here so she could open back up. She's actually the one who renamed it. Kind of like a caterpillar becoming a butterfly.

She said she wanted to turn it from something ugly to a beautiful place where guys would be proud to take their dates." He winks at me then glances around the small bar. "I have to say, there have been fewer bar fights since she became the owner."

"Wow," I gasp. Seriously, I can't even imagine the state this room was in before she took over. "That's actually pretty amazing. If she ever wants to grow, I might know a few people that could make it happen. People in Austin would love this place." I tap my finger against my chin, my mind going a million miles an hour. "On second thought, she shouldn't fix the outside. It helps with the name. That is the old, and the inside is what came of it."

"Damn, Stella." Johnny shakes his head and laughs. "Are you sure you aren't in marketing? You kind of went off with that idea."

"Eh," I tilt my head. "It's not too far off from what I do now. Except my job is more of making sure shit gets done when it's supposed to."

"Well, I think you went down the wrong career path. But I'll introduce you and Angie when she comes back with our drinks."

"How long have you been working on cars?" I mean if we're talking jobs and day to day life, it's time I asked him.

"Since I was eighteen." Johnny rubs his chin, thinking. "Technically before that. I used to help my grandpa when he was alive. He always told me it was a good idea to know how to work on your own vehicle. Then I wouldn't have to depend on someone else to fix it."

"I feel like maybe that was directed at me."

"Not at all. Most people don't know where to locate the oil dipstick. Gramps made sure that I knew how to do at least the basics before I was even allowed to put the key in the ignition. Honestly, I can't think of anything else I'd do instead. I love working on cars. I feel like I'm doing something that helps others."

Angie approaches our table with a drink in each hand. "Here y'all go. Are you ready to order?"

"Yep," Johnny grabs the menu I set down. "But first, I'd like to introduce you to my *date*." His eyes gleam knowing that every reference to this being a date is getting under my skin. "Angie, this is Stella. She's here for a while to get the distribution center up and running. Stella, this is the owner of this fine establishment, Angie."

"It's nice to meet you," Angie holds her hand out to me.

I take it in mine, and I'm surprised to find that the palms of her hands are rough. She must do a lot of the work around here. Most people I know that own businesses sit around and let others do the grunt work. "It's nice to meet you, too. I love how you've decorated everything. It's completely unexpected."

"Thanks," she blushes. "I need to work on the outside, but it's all coming together."

"Actually," I interrupt. "I have a few ideas I want to run by you when you have a chance."

"I'd love that." Angie smiles. Someone calls her name, and she turns searching for the person. "I'll get you my number before you leave. What did y'all decided to eat?"

Johnny answers first, "Wings."

"And what about you Stella?"

"I'll have what he's having." I grin at Johnny. "He said they are the best in town."

"Alrighty, I'll get them out as soon as they are ready. I need to go see what this guy wants." She rushes in the direction of the man calling her name.

"Where's the rest of the staff?" I whisper.

"She doesn't usually have them all working during the week. She saves most of them for the weekend."

"I see."

"It hasn't been long since she re-opened the place. She doesn't want to jump all in just in case it folds."

"I'll help her get this place filled to the brim with patrons."

Johnny grabs my hand and squeezes it. "How are you going to have time to do your job, date me, *and* help Angie?"

"I have my ways." I pull my hand from his. "Besides, who said I was going to date you?"

"It's no use fighting the inevitable."

"The wings were everything you promised them to be." We're walking out of the bar and to our cars. As skeptical as I was when I decided to meet Johnny here, I don't want the night to end.

"I told you. Maybe one day you'll listen to what I have to say." He bumps his shoulder into mine.

This is a bad idea. I know it is down to my core, but I can't fight my attraction to him. Besides, I can casually date. I'm a freaking adult. "What if I said, I'm leaning more into the yes column when it comes to dating you?"

"I would ask you to come over because I'm not ready to tell you goodnight." Hearing that makes me tingle. He's definitely been pushing for this and with all of his annoying comments that push all the right buttons. Even though it's terrifying that it's *me* he wants, I am starting to feel the same way. However, I'm not going to give in that easily. If I just give in, he'll come to expect it all the time. Though he may be bringing out a new side of me, I am not going to stop guarding my heart with the ferocity of a dog protecting its bone.

"I'll have to raincheck on tonight. But I'm not opposed to seeing you again." I grab the car keys from my pocket, and unlock the door. "Maybe I'll come over this weekend, and you can also show me the progress on my car."

"It's a date," he smirks and leans toward me. "But don't think you're getting out of here without me kissing you."

My back is against the car door, his fingers tangled in my long tresses, and his lips seared to my own. If he doesn't stop kissing me like this, I'll cave way too soon and go home with him right now.

His tongue sweeps across my lips before slipping into my mouth. My knees buckle and I wrap my arms around his waist to steady myself. Oh damn, he knows how to use his tongue, and I can only imagine what it would feel like pressed against my—.

My thoughts are interrupted as he pulls away. *Of course.* "Goodnight, Stella," he whispers into the night air. Talk about a complete shift in mood. "Text me when you get home so I know you made it."

I am left speechless and wanting more as he moves away from me. But I am not too stunned to miss the way he readjusts his pants as he takes a step back. Nodding, I open the car door and slide into the seat. "Goodnight Johnny," I mutter into the now vacant space where he was standing moments ago.

I'm going to need a cold shower, or two, and my trusty BOB.

Chapter Eighteen

I THOUGHT my office in Austin was quiet, it's nothing compared to this. I'll be happy when we fill this building with employees because right now…it's a little creepy. The construction workers are finished inside, and making the finishing touches that need to take place outside.

"Yes, Mr. Jones," I say into the receiver of my phone. "I'll need those tables here by the twentieth at four p.m.."

"Is there any way we can drop them off sooner?" He sounds impatient, but I told him the date and time in the email I originally sent on Monday.

I guess it wouldn't hurt anything to get them here earlier. It would give me extra time to set up for the Job Fair. "Yes, what time are you thinking?"

"Early morning, probably around nine."

"That sounds great. Just knock on the door for the dock when you get here."

"Yes ma'am. I'll see you then." Mr. Jones hangs up before I can say goodbye. Is it wrong that I pictured him tipping a cowboy hat when he said "yes, ma'am"? I know it's a stereotype, but I wouldn't be surprised to find that people around here actually do it. It's part of my vision of small towns. I remember being shocked that my aunts and uncles waved to everyone they passed on the road, even when they didn't know them. It's such a weird concept to me.

Pulling up the app on my phone that holds my checklist for the Job Fair I have to put on, I sigh. There's still so much shit I need to do, and I have no idea how I'm going to do it all on my own. I wonder if Mr. Hart would approve a request for an assistant while I'm down here. I add a line on the list to email Rosie about it tomorrow. I would do it now, but talking with Mr. Jones wore me out. It took forever to get him on the topic of why *he* called me. I'm beginning to wonder if I am actually cut out for this job, or if I'm reaching too high with my goals of the promotion. Would it be the worst thing to be content with the position I have now? It could be worse. I could be like Tiffany and flit from job to job.

With my fingers on my temples, and my eyes closed, I attempt to rub away the stress starting to weigh on me. *You can do this, Stella. Don't let some grumpy old man break your spirit.* My phone ringing sounds like a siren in the silent building, and my knee bangs against the desk at the sound. *Son of a bitch.* I answer it without looking at who is calling. "Hello."

"What's up girl? How's small town life treating you?" Tiffany's voice comes through the receiver. Why is she calling me in the middle of the day?

"Shouldn't you be at work?"

"No," she draws out. "It's after six. Are *you* still at work?"

"Shit. I didn't even realize that much time has passed." Maybe that's why Mr. Jones was in a foul mood. He was ready to go home for the day. "How's everything back home? It's been over a week since I was there, and you assholes haven't filled me in on anything."

"Same old shit, different day." She pauses for a few seconds. "I *have* been staying at your apartment, though. My roommate is driving me crazy."

"Tiff, I don't think you've had one that doesn't annoy you. What did Bri do now?" I laugh. I can't help it. Tiffany approaches finding a roommate the same way she dates. Fast decisions without knowing anything about them.

"She threw out my fucking food." Her screeching is high enough to wake the dead.

"Was it old?"

"There may have been one or two things that needed to be thrown out," she concedes.

If I had to guess, it was more than that, but she's on a tirade. The last thing I feel like dealing with is getting bitched at for defending Bri. "Don't y'all have a rule about touching each other's food?"

"Yeah, but her neat freak self obviously doesn't know how to abide by it."

"Maybe it's time you found a new roommate."

"Already on it, Cuz." I can hear her smile through the phone and a pang of homesickness hits me in the gut. As much as I appreciate this opportunity, being away from my cousins has been terrible. "She's looking for a new place, and I've already put out an ad."

Oh Lord, this isn't going to go well unless Audrey helps with the process. "Do you want to send me a list of the applicants when they come in? I can check them out for you." Anything to keep her from finding someone that might hurt her in some way. She has zero self-preservation skills.

"Thanks, but no. I've got it under control."

"Oh yeah? How?"

"I'll see what my gut says when I meet them to tour the place. If I get bad vibes, they are an automatic no."

I snort. "One day that gut feeling is going to get your ass in serious trouble." I gather my things and shove them in my bag. I should stay to finalize more things for the Job Fair, but I promised myself I'd be out of here at five. No more work for today. It's nice being able set my own schedule without Mr. Granger breathing down my neck.

"Maybe, but I'm still alive." I imagine her shrugging as she says it. Sometimes, I wish I could be more like her and just take everything one day at a time. I mean I'm sort of doing that with Johnny, but it's terrifying.

"Shockingly," I mutter.

"Don't be bitter because you don't know how to have fun."

"I know how to have fun," I scoff as I walk out of the building and lock up. "I'm just careful about it."

"Prove it." Ugh, how am I supposed to do that? "Did you take the hot mechanic up on his offer?"

"Actually, yes."

"Seriously?" She laughs so loud I have to pull the phone away from my ear. "I didn't think you had it in you," she says between gasps. *Gee, thanks for the vote of confidence.*

"Whatever, asshole. He's fun to hang out with. I'm supposed to see him this weekend."

"Is 'hanging out' the new phrase for having all the sex?"

"No, we haven't done that…yet. But we've had dinner twice."

"Ugh," Tiffany groans. "You're such a goody two shoes. I'm going to start calling you Audrey before long."

"I don't have to screw every guy I come in contact with like someone else I know." I regret the words as soon as they leave my mouth. "I'm so sorry Tiff."

"It's all good. I'm confident in my sexy times." She pauses, "I need to get going anyway."

Fuck. "Okay. Love you."

"Love you, too." The line goes dead.

I need to figure out a way to apologize. I didn't mean to say it, but why was she on my ass about this whole Johnny thing? My fingers itch to call her back, but she needs time to cool off. I'll call tomorrow. If there's one thing I can count on with Tiffany, it's that she doesn't hold grudges.

I really need a drink after this insane day. It's a good thing I know the perfect bar.

Chapter Nineteen

OUT OF THE Ashes is busier than it was when I came with Johnny. All the tables are filled with people chatting and enjoying a night out. Instead of waiting for a table to open up, I head straight to the bar. There's no use wasting an entire table on one person. Besides, maybe I'll be able to talk to Angie more about this place. It doesn't appear as if she needs help filling the seats but she could easily turn this into a must stop location for people coming through. Hell, she could help put Asheville on the map.

"Hi, Stella," Angie calls from the other side of the bar as I take my seat. It's loud and I can barely hear her over the music and chatter. "I didn't expect to see you back here so soon."

"It's been a long day," I sigh. "Any chance I can get a whiskey sour?"

"Absolutely. I'll bring it over in just a bit. Let me take care of this customer really quick." She finishes mixing a drink for someone directly in front of her. She's fast, I'll give her that. She barely has to watch what she's doing. If I were doing that, there'd be liquor all over the floor, and probably on me. I could never in a million years work behind a bar.

Angie walks toward me with my drink in hand. "Here you go, Hon. Do you want anything to eat?" She sets the glass down.

My stomach growls at the mention of food. I can't remember if I even took a lunch break today, but from the sound of it, I didn't. "Actually, yeah. Can I get an order of those wings I had the other day?"

"I'll get that in for you." She wipes the counter down before turning towards the kitchen. "I'll come chat as soon as it slows down. We're usually not this busy."

"It's a good thing, though. Lots of business means you can hire more people to take some of the burden off of yourself."

"That is so very true. I'll have those wings out soon." She rushes off to put in my order and wait on other people.

She's sweet and definitely someone I would be friends with if we lived in the same town. Why is it that a small part of me feels like I'm cheating on my cousins just thinking about this? Logically, I know we should stop being so codependent. Maybe then we could have lives instead of it revolving around each other. *Ugh.* Why am I being so maudlin tonight?

I'm not usually one to overthink things when it comes to them. Other parts of my life, yes. But the three of us have always been a given. I guess it has something to do with being alone for the first time in years that's giving me perspective. It's actually kind of nice not being with them all the time. Or dealing with one of Tiffany's tantrums on a daily basis.

It's like my own sort of vacation from my normal life,

and figuring out who I am on my own. I lift my glass to my lips savoring the realization.

"Is this seat taken?" A deep voice whispers next to my ear. *His* deep voice. My glass almost slips from my grasp.

Amber liquid sloshes over the edge onto my fingers as I steady the glass. "You scared the hell out of me, Johnny. What are you doing here?"

"Probably the same thing as you. Getting a bite to eat, and having a few drinks." The smug grin on his face makes me roll my eyes. He's such a smart ass.

"Thank you for stating the obvious. How did you even know I was here? Are you stalking me?" I poke his chest. Hopefully by now he knows I'm only kidding. "You're making me rethink dating you if you're going to have serial killer behavior."

"Don't worry," he chuckles. "I'm not going to hack you into tiny pieces." He leans against the bar, forearms holding him up. "I'm here with a guy from work. Reaf and his wife trade nights when they hang out with friends. She gets one night a week for book club, and he gets one night."

"Wait, there's a book club that meets here?" I take a drink of my whiskey. "I love reading. Though, I can't remember the last time I actually had a chance to pick up a book."

"Hold your horses, Stella. I'm not sure how much they actually talk about books." He nods his head toward the front door. A guy who looks like he's barely out of high school is talking to the young woman at the hosts stand. "He says they mostly get together at a coffee shop and gossip about what's going on in their lives while drinking an insane amount of caffeine."

"Is he even old enough to drink?" I glance over Johnny's shoulder at the guy walking toward us. "He looks like a baby."

"If he wasn't, he wouldn't be here. I was actually supposed to hang out with him the night I found you stranded on the side of the road. His little girl was sick, and he had to cancel."

"I guess it's a good thing your plans changed. Otherwise, we wouldn't have met." I drop my voice a few octaves trying to sound sexy. His answering smirk tells me just how ridiculous I sound.

Reaf reaches us and holds out his hand. "You must be Stella." I place my hand in his and turn a questioning gaze toward Johnny. "He talks about you…a lot. He also said he got rid of a snake for you."

My cheeks warm. I hope he didn't tell him *everything* about that morning. Like the fact that we were both almost naked, and eyeing each other like people who've spent ages circling their feelings rather than two people that have barely met. "Yep," I try to hide my embarrassment. "I never had that issue before. At least, not where I live."

"Welcome to the country," Reaf laughs. "You never know what's going to show up." Johnny's eyes haven't left my face since Reaf started talking. Reaf notices, and backs away. "I'll let you catch up. Johnny, I'll text you when our table is ready."

"Thanks man." Johnny doesn't spare his friend a glance. "What are you doing tomorrow night?"

"Nothing that I know of. Why?"

"A few of us are going to a bonfire. Do you want to go with me?"

Bonfires really aren't my thing. Not that I've ever been to one. I just know what I've seen on TV and in the movies. It doesn't look like something I'd enjoy. On the other hand, I told Tiff I was capable of having unplanned fun. Turning this down would be the exact opposite. "Is it okay that I'm being invited last minute? I don't want to step on any toes."

"It's fine." He leans closer. "It's not a formal event. Just a few old friends getting together, drinking a few beers, and relaxing."

"Oh, okay. Sure, I'm game." I want to tell him it's my first one, but he'll think I'm crazy. "What time do I need to show up? And what's the address?"

"Meet me at my house around seven. Is that good with you?"

Reaf waves his arms to get Johnny's attention, in lieu of texting. "It looks like our table is ready. I'll see you tomorrow night. Text me when you get home."

"Okay." He leans in and gives me a soft kiss on my cheek. "I'll see you then."

Angie shows up with my wings as Johnny walks away. "He's got it bad for you. In all the years I've known him, he's never paid so much attention to a woman."

"Why not?" That's shocking to me, I figured he'd be a ladies' man.

"I don't know. I haven't seen him in any sort of relationship since high school."

That's interesting. I wipe the sticky spot where my whiskey spilled over, and lean my arms on the bar. "What happened to make that his last real relationship?"

She glances at me and then back at him. "That's not really my story to tell." Her knuckles tap on the bartop. "Do you need another drink?"

"Um, yes. Thank you." I watch her walk away to mix me another drink. She didn't take the opportunity to spill all the juicy details about Johnny. I remember my cousins telling me about how much shit people talked about each other in their small town. Angie definitely has my respect for keeping her lips sealed.

My thoughts are all over the place, and I don't notice the drink now in front until Angie speaks. "Let me know if you need anything else. We can talk business after I close if you're still here."

"Thanks." I look behind me in the direction Johnny and Reaf walked. He definitely piqued my interest more than he did before. Maybe he has more layers than I originally thought. And maybe my heart is getting a lot more than it bargained for.

Chapter Twenty

NOPE. These aren't nerves racing through my body. It's just exhaustion from the day. That's why I can't decide what to wear to the bonfire. I should call Tiff and ask for her opinion, but I'm not going to. She still hasn't texted me after what I said to her yesterday. Not that I blame her. I definitely put my foot in my mouth. Maybe I'll drive down there and see her. There has to be something I can do to get her to forgive me. Or, at least talk to me.

My phone vibrates across the dresser and I rush to it, hoping my thoughts conjured a call from Tiffany. It's not her, though. Johnny's name flashes across the screen. "Hello."

"Hey, Stella." Loud music is playing in the background. "Are you still coming?"

"Yeah," I look around my room at the piles of clothes littering the floor and bed. "I'm getting dressed. Why?"

"It's almost eight, and I was getting worried." He pauses and sucks in a breath before letting it out. "But if you're not dressed, it sounds like your house may be more fun."

"Very funny. I didn't realize the time. I'll be over in fifteen minutes."

Johnny chuckles, and the sound sends a shiver down my body. Just his voice sends me into a tailspin. "Slow down. There's no rush. I was only checking in."

"I feel horrible." Dammit. How did I lose track of time? I grab a few clothes from the pile on my bed, not bothering to see what they are. "I'll be there soon." I don't give him a chance to say anything else before hanging up. I have ten minutes to get dressed and do something with my hair.

Dressed and hair in a high ponytail, I walk out of the house, locking the door behind me. It's a good thing he lives so close.

Johnny's truck is parked outside of his house when I pull up, but the house is dark. Maybe someone picked him up. He must have gotten tired of waiting. I'd meet him there, but I don't know where this bonfire is happening. He only told me to meet him at his house. Why is it so eerie? He really needs to get his porch light fixed because sitting in complete darkness makes me uneasy.

I grab my purse and dig around for my phone. I know it's in here somewhere. There's a possibility that he's not too far away and can turn around to come get me. My finger is hovering over his name when there's a knock on my window, and I jump. The phone flies out of my hand, landing somewhere in the backseat.

I'm scrambling to get my seatbelt off as someone begins to open the door. All I can think is that I need a weapon, and the only thing I have is a travel coffee mug. This is not how I imagined my night turning out. "Stella?" His voice stops me in my tracks, and I face the now open car door. "Are you okay?"

"Does it look like I'm okay?" I huff. "You scared the

hell out of me. I was about to call you. I didn't expect you to sneak up on me like a crazy person."

He winces. "Sorry, I thought you saw me walking toward your car."

"In the dark?" I shake my head. "You could have been a deranged killer for all I know."

"You might want to lay off the horror movies," he laughs. "This is a small town and we know everyone here."

"Why aren't any of your lights on?"

"I was waiting in the truck. It seemed easier to meet you out here rather than invite you in only to leave again."

I guess that makes sense. It does nothing to quell my racing heart, though. He is right in one aspect. I need to stop watching scary movies period. Even better, Hollywood needs to stop setting horror movies in rural areas. Rather than let him know just how badly he's scared me; I steer the conversation in a different direction. "How far away is the bonfire?"

"Not far. It's actually on the back end of my property."

"How much land do you freaking have?"

"More than enough. My grandpa used to let the high school kids from Asheville go out there to hang out so at least they had somewhere safe to do whatever teenagers do." He shrugs and takes a step back, giving me space to get out of the car. "It's the perfect place. There aren't any buildings, or neighbors, and if anyone drinks more than they should, they are able to stay the night out there."

"What?" I shriek. "People actually do that?"

"Yep. We *are* in the country. Most people out here grew up camping. It's nothing they aren't used to."

"Y'all are weird."

"What do you do when you go out and drink too much? Surely you don't drive after that."

"I'm not a moron. I usually Uber wherever I need to go to avoid driving at all costs. Or if the place is close, I walk."

He nods his head, deep in thought. "That doesn't sound any safer to me."

"It's why I usually go places with Audrey and Tiffany. People tend to leave you alone if you're in a group."

"So, safety in numbers?"

"Exactly." I get out of the car and the heel of my boot sinks into the dirt. I groan. These boots were obviously a bad choice. I just wanted to give myself some height. I feel tiny compared to Johnny, and if I'm taller...it makes kissing him that much easier.

"Are you ready to head to the fire?" Johnny holds his hand out, waiting for me to grab it.

I slip my hand into his, and move to close the car door. "Lead the way." He walks me to the passenger side of his truck, opens the door, and helps me inside. "We're driving?"

"It's faster than walking." He glances down at my boots. "And I have a feeling your feet will thank me in the end."

I have no idea how I didn't hear the music from Johnny's house. The bass is pounding through the windows before we've even gotten to the other cars parked in the pasture. I can see outlines of people milling around a fire blazing at its full glory. My palms are beginning to sweat as fear seeps in.

I don't know anyone here aside from Johnny. Meeting new people is something that's always been hard for me. I'm not necessarily shy, but Audrey and Tiffany are my people. They are the ones I do everything with. There's never been a need to find other people with them always around.

"Is it too late to do something else tonight?" I ask as Johnny parks the truck and faces me.

"Don't be nervous. These are good people. You'll have no problem fitting in. But, if you really want to go back to the house, or go home, I can take you back." With this, he begins to calm my nerves. He barely even knows me, yet he knows how to deal with my crazy.

I stare out the window, watching his friends, and trying so hard to tamp down the fear that they won't like me. The need to bail almost has me asking him to go back, but I need to do this. I need to stop being so wrapped up in my cousins lives that it stifles the chance to forge new friendships. "It's okay. I can do this."

He leans closer to me, placing his hand on my cheek. "If you feel uncomfortable at any time, just say the word and we'll go back to my place." His lips touch mine in soft and reassuring kiss.

"Let's do this." The words are more for me than him. The same thing I repeat to myself when I have a gigantic task ahead of me that needs to be tackled. Johnny gets out of the truck and comes around the front to open the door for me. His eyes never leaving mine, and some of the fear I had about being here melts away.

We walk hand in hand, toward the fire. All at once everyone stops their conversations and stares at us. I feel like a science experiment on display, waiting for the teacher to tell everyone what went wrong. "Everyone, this is Stella. Stella, this is everyone." He waves his hand across the expanse of open field.

Some wave awkwardly, but one person runs up and wraps her arms around me. "I'm so glad you made it."

"I didn't know you were going to be here, Angie." Relief spreads through my body. At least, I know two people here.

"Yep," she nods. "I had one of the guys I can rely on handle the bar tonight. Sometimes we all need a little time to take a break from adulting."

"Honestly, adulting is overrated," I laugh. "We spend our entire lives wanting to grow up, and realize when we're older that we want those simpler things."

"Girl, you're not telling me anything I don't already know." She walks us toward an ice chest, and Johnny goes over to a group of guys. "Want a beer?"

Beer isn't usually my drink of choice, but it's not like there's a stocked bar with liquor in the middle of a field. "Sure, whatever you have is fine." She grabs a bottle and opens it, handing it off to me. "Thanks." But before I can bring the bottle to my lips, she shoves a wedge of lime into the bottle.

"It helps with the taste," she grins.

I take a sip, and I'm surprised to find I like it. It's not like I've never had beer before, I've just never acquired the taste for it. I much prefer wine or whiskey. "It's good."

"I knew you'd like it." She rests her hand on my arm, and nods toward two camp chairs sitting by the fire. "Johnny set up some chairs for y'all, but since he's not using them, let's go chat."

"Sounds good to me. I'm just happy I know someone besides Johnny."

"These folks are harmless. You have nothing to worry

about," she laughs. "We all grew up together, and a lot of them stayed close to home. It's one of the amazing things about living in a small town. We're all like family."

"That's pretty awesome. I didn't have a ton of friends in high school. I mostly talked to my cousins when we'd get out or on the weekends. I'd visit them every summer and during any breaks I had from school." Looking back, it's kind of sad just how much I relied on Audrey and Tiffany. I was in a ton of clubs during school with every opportunity to make friends, but I didn't. The one friend I thought I had turned out to be a horrible person and gossiped about me behind my back. Thus, began my lack of trust in people in general. If they weren't family, they didn't really matter to me.

"I love that you're so close with your cousins." She takes the chair closest to the fire and I sit in the one next to her. It's insanely hot, and I'm wondering why people have bonfires when it's still relatively warm outside. "I don't have many cousins, but the ones I do have…we don't get along at all."

"That sucks." And it does. I've gone a full twenty-four hours without knowing if Tiffany is still mad at me, and it's messing with me head. "I can't imagine not talking to my cousins. We are pretty much inseparable. In fact, when they heard about my temporary relocation for this job, they were not as happy as I would have liked."

"Oh," her face falls. "You aren't here permanently?"

"No. I work in management for a property firm in Austin. They are the ones opening the distribution center outside of Asheville. I'm here to make sure everything is good to go. Then I'll be going back home."

"Oh. That's good. I assumed most companies would hire that out."

"Most do, but the CEO of ours said I'd get a promotion if it opens without hitch. It's one I've been eyeing for a year, so here I am."

"I have no doubt you'll get it done." She smiles. I feel like she really means it. It's not a backhanded compliment, and she's not saying it just to make me feel better.

"Thanks. It's a lot more work than I thought it would be, though."

"It seems like everything in life is a lot harder than we think."

"So true." I raise my bottle, and tap it against hers. "To kicking ass and taking names in whatever we choose to do." Both of us take a drink and fall into easy conversation about nothing important.

I've lost track of Johnny, and that doesn't bother me in the slightest. I'm making a friend, and hopefully it will be a relationship that lasts long after I head back to Austin when this job is over.

I'm in the middle of telling her what I think she should do with marketing for the bar when her eyes widen. "Oh, shit. This isn't going to be good."

I follow her gaze toward the shiny black car making its way onto the pasture. "Who is it?"

She looks at me, then back at the car, now parking. "The girl who broke Johnny's heart."

Chapter Twenty-One

Not good, not good. Why wouldn't Johnny tell me that his ex was going to be here? A tall brunette woman steps out of the sleek car, and walks toward the fire. There is a confidence in her stride made easier by the fact she didn't wear boots with heels to a bonfire. Her clothes are so tight they cling to her skin. Her very demeanor reminds me of Tiffany when she's looking to hook up, and I know right then and there that I'm screwed.

I watch as she walks up to Johnny from behind and wraps her arms around him. When he realizes it's not me, his body stiffens. He breaks away from the woman behind him, and turns to face her. I have no idea what his expression is, but his hands are balled into fists. "What the fuck are you doing here?" His voice isn't loud, but the anger wrapped around the words stops all conversation.

"I heard there was a bonfire tonight, and I knew it could only be happening here." Her tone is sugary sweet as she hungrily eyes Johnny up and down.

"I'm guessing she's not supposed to be here?" I whisper, hoping Angie can hear me.

I catch her shaking her head out of the corner of my eye. "Nope. Hell, I didn't even know she was back in town."

"Any chance she'll leave?" Please say yes. I am fighting with the urge to march over and claim Johnny as mine so she'll back off. But I stop myself. We've only been on a couple of dates, and I know I don't have the right to make a claim over him. Or do I?

"I'm sure he'll ask her to, but Sarah will just sweet talk her way into staying."

Fuck. This is not good. Before I realize what I'm doing, I'm standing and making my way toward Johnny. I slip my arm into his and lean my head on his shoulder. I hold my free hand out, trying to defuse the situation. "Hi, I'm Stella."

She doesn't even glance my way. Instead she focuses on Johnny. "I hope it's okay if I hang out for a while. There's nothing to do at my parents' house, and it's so good to see old friends."

I don't like the way she says friends. Hell, I don't like the way she didn't even acknowledge my existence. I glance up at Johnny, waiting to see what he'll say. "Do whatever you want, Sarah," he spits out. "I'm not going to cause a scene. Just stay away from me."

He doesn't say anything else. He shifts his arm until it's wrapped around my side, and turns us until we're facing the other direction, leading us toward the chairs I was just occupying which Angie has conveniently left open.

The silence is getting to me. He's angry, and if the vibe I'm getting off of him is any indication, he has every right to be. His ex just crashed the small party he's having on his own property. "I'm guessing you two know each other?" I do my best to make it sound lighthearted, but I know he can hear the fear and tension in my voice.

"Yep." He grabs my unfinished beer and takes a swig, making a face. It has to be hot by now. Angie and I were so wrapped up in our conversation that I completely forgot about it. "She's my ex, and makes my life hell anytime she comes into town."

"I'm sorry." I glance toward the people talking now that the awkwardness has ended. Sarah is glaring at me, and a ball of unease settles in my stomach. I have a feeling she's going to make my life hell, too. This whole thing with Johnny is supposed to be easy, something we can both walk away from. Now, it's getting complicated.

I shiver despite the warmth. "Want to get out of here?"

His shoulders sag in relief. "Yes. My place, or yours?"

"Your house is closer." Right now, I only want away from the scary lady. I have a feeling he needs to be away from her, too.

"Let's go, then." He helps me up, and we start walking toward the truck. He's quiet until we run into Angie. "We're gonna head out. Feel free to shut this down whenever you want."

"We'll clear out of here soon." Her eyes shift to the vicinity Sarah is in. "I don't know who told her we were all out here, but I'll find out." Her eyes are on me, and she smiles.

"Thanks, Ang. We'll stop by the bar tomorrow." I guess he's already lining up our next date. I'm not upset about it, but I definitely need to find out what the hell went on with him and Sarah before anything else happens.

Johnny's house is now a beacon in the dark night. I swear he turned on every single light. He even grabbed a lightbulb and replaced the one on the porch. "Are you trying to protect yourself from the things that go bump in the night?"

"What?" He looks at me, confused. I point to all the light spilling into every room. "Oh, she just makes me uneasy."

"What happened with the two of you?" I don't want to know all the details but I need to know what might be coming at me when I'm not paying attention.

"Oh, you know, the same thing that makes up all tragic small-town love stories." He sits down on the sofa beside me, absentmindedly running his fingertips along my leg. "We were high school sweethearts. She wanted bigger and better things. I wanted to stay here. There was no in-between for her. I either went with her or I was going to lose her forever. I lost her. Then after she left, I found out she was screwing around on me. Any regret on following her was gone after I knew the truth."

"Why is she here now?" That must be why he doesn't want anything with strings attached. I totally respect him for that. He knows what he's capable of, and it sounds like trusting people is an issue we both have in common.

"I honestly have no clue." He turns until his back is up against the arm rest, and pulls me until I'm laying halfway on him and the couch. The steady thump of his heart is calming. "She doesn't visit very often, but when she does, I swear her only goal in life is to make mine miserable and try to screw with my head."

At least I know he doesn't want anything to do with her. If I would have heard any doubt in his words, I would have to end whatever we are. I don't need, nor want, that kind of drama in my life. "Was she always like that?"

"Honestly, yeah. I was just too stupid in love to realize it. No matter how many times my friends tried to warn me," he looks down at me and smiles. "I should listen to them more often, though. Angie really likes you."

"I like her too. She kept me company until shit hit the fan. It was nice to not feel like a tagalong or outsider. It honestly felt like we'd been friends for years."

"I'm happy for that. She's one of my closest friends. Our moms are best friends so we've known each other since we were in diapers."

"I got that feeling about her. She's very protective of you."

"Only because she doesn't want someone coming around and fucking me over the way Sarah did." The room falls silent after that. She is to him what my cousins are to me. He picks the remote off of the coffee table. "Want to watch a movie? I feel like maybe I need to turn this date around from the shit show it was back there."

"Sounds good to me." Just then a thought hits me, and I'm worried his bitchy ex will show up unannounced. "Will everyone be passing through your driveway when they leave?" I really don't want anything to interrupt our night more than it already has.

"Nah, Angie will make everyone leave through the gate that leads to a small access road." He starts scrolling through the guide menu on the tv. "Is there anything in particular you want to watch?"

"Nope, I'm good with anything that isn't sappy." He pauses on a sci-fi movie.

While I'm a huge fan of vampires, witches, and all that other stuff, science fiction has never been my thing. I don't say anything, though. I choose to snuggle as close to him as possible and watch the movie. With each minute that passes, all the uncertainty from Sarah showing up slips away. I let myself be held by this man that makes me feel everything I shouldn't. The only thing that would make it better is a bowl of popcorn.

My arm between us is falling asleep. I shift my body until I'm lying on my side in front of him and his back is against the sofa. His arm wraps around me to pull me closer to him until my back is touching him. His fingers rub gently along my waist where my shirt has shifted, exposing a tiny slip of skin, and heat races through my body.

His rough fingers are creating the perfect friction against my smooth skin. I shift my legs trying to ease the tension pooling below. All it does is turn me on even more than I am. He slides his other arm underneath me and his hand cups my breast. Gently squeezing until I'm all but panting.

As impossible as it seems, he pulls me even closer to him, and his hardness presses into my lower back. That's all the confirmation I need to know that he wants me as badly as I want him. I wiggle my ass, and he groans. The surge of glee I feel boosts my confidence. My hand slides past his until it reaches my pants button. I undo the button and slide my zipper down giving him permission to go lower. To make me come alive. Anticipation building. Waiting for him to make the next move.

Johnny's hand slides down. His fingertips brushing the top of my panties, and I shiver, before he pauses. "Not like this."

I suck in a breath. "What?"

"We aren't going to have sex for the first time on this ratty couch like a couple of horny teenagers." He slides out from behind me and grabs my hand. "Come one. My bed is much more comfortable."

I allow him to pull me up when he pulls me in for a deep toe-curling kiss. Not wanting to waste any time, I head in the direction of his bedroom. I guess that is one benefit of my snooping the first night I was here.

With each step we take another layer of clothing off as it hits the floor. The look in his eyes is pure lust, and it is better than any foreplay I could imagine. I've never been as bold as I am right now, showing him what I want. Pulling him toward what I know is going to be an amazing end to the night. As my legs hit the edge of his bed, I fall backward. My bra and panties the only clothing I have left. He lifts himself on top of me, kissing every bare inch of my skin he can—any doubts I had about what we were going to do or be to each other melt away.

Chapter Twenty-Two

I SQUINT as morning sunshine slips between the blinds. Ugh, why is the sun up? For a minute, I forget where I am, but quickly I take stock of my surroundings. *Dammit.* I was supposed to go home last night, not shack up with the hot mechanic. Not that I'm complaining. Last night was the best sex I think I've ever had.

Rolling over, I slide my arm over the other side of the bed. It's empty. *What the hell?* You're not supposed to ditch the chick you screwed in your own house. I hear shuffling coming from the front of the house, and search for my clothes. Fuck, they are scattered throughout the house. I don't want to walk out there with a sheet wrapped around my body.

Opening his closet door, I grab the first shirt I see. I pull it over my head and walk out of his room. Johnny is pacing back and forth in the kitchen, running his fingers through his hair over and over again. Does he not want me here? "If you wanted me to leave this morning, you could have woken me up."

He turns around and his eyes go wide, trailing his gaze

up and down my body. "You look fucking amazing in my work shirt."

I look down, and realize a Small Town Automotive patch sewn above the pocket. My cheeks warm, and I groan. "Sorry. I'll go find my clothes."

I turn to leave the kitchen, but he grabs my arm and pulls me toward him. "Don't be ridiculous. The only place it would look better is on the floor." He places a kiss on my neck, then my jawbone, and works his way to my earlobe. "Hell, maybe you can leave it on until we're done."

I suck in a breath at his words, and relish the feel of his lips on my body. Then I remember his pacing when I walked in. "Why were you walking a hole through the floor?"

That snaps him out of his sexy talk, and he runs his hand through his hair again. He pulls back and hurries to the refrigerator. "Are you hungry? I can whip us up something to eat."

Leaning against the wall, I tap my foot, and cross my arms over my chest. His shirt rises, and his eyes shoot to where the hem of it ends. "What aren't you telling me?"

"I don't know what you're talking about."

"You're acting like a kid who has done something wrong and doesn't want to fess up to his parents."

He leans against the fridge, and hits the back of his head on the door. "There may be a teensy tiny problem with your car."

"Is it going to cost more than you thought? It's not a big deal if it is."

"Yes, but I don't need you to pay for it because it's my fault."

I whip my head back. His fault? He's supposed to be fixing it. "What did you do?" I'm trying really hard to not accuse him of anything, but he's acting cagey and I need to know why.

"Well," he shuffles to his right until he has a clear path out of the kitchen. "There may have been an incident."

"What kind of incident?"

"Well, you know how you had a back bumper?" He waits for me to nod. "You're getting a brand new one."

"Did you back into something?"

"Not exactly." One shoulder rises until it's almost touching his head. "When I was working on the front bumper, and headlight, I had it lifted up a bit. And well, apparently, I forgot to shift the car from neutral to park, and when I leaned on it…it rolled out of the garage and into the fence."

"What?" I shriek. I should have had him tow it to a dealer to get it looked at, but he was so earnest about fixing it. "How bad is it?"

He shrugs. "It's not horrible, but it's not pretty."

"Show me." I storm to the front door, not caring that I'm still wearing only his shirt and no shoes. I march onto the porch, and I'm about to take a step off when he tugs me back.

"Don't you think you should put on some pants?" He's looking toward the road, determining if anyone can see me.

"Not until you show me my baby."

"Fine," he huffs. He leads me to the garage walking on the side that faces the road, and then behind me when we turn toward the garage.

The dying grass digs into my feet, and I wish for a second that I would have at least put on some damn shoes. My tender feet can't handle this nonsense, and I wince with every step I take.

Right before we get to the garage door, Johnny stops me in my tracks. "Promise you won't freak out."

"I'm not a hundred percent sure I can promise that."

"Okay," he sighs. "I'll open the door for you, and I won't come in until I know you won't chop my balls off."

Smart man. He opens the side door, and lets me pass in front of him. True to his word, he doesn't follow. My baby is sitting next to an old rusted car, and I almost cry at the sight of her. I'm grateful to Johnny's mom for letting me use her extra car, but there's nothing like driving your own.

I stare at the front of the car and take stock of the work he was doing on the front end. That part looks almost finished. It will only take a few more hours to be back to the condition it was in when I drove it off the lot. The back is the problem he mentioned, though. I take a deep breath, run my fingers along the side of my car, and walk to the backend. Holy shit. He wasn't lying. The bumper is completely gone. The plus side…the metal thingy it attaches to is still there, but the bumper lies, discarded, on the floor.

"Is it okay for me to come in?" He calls from outside. "If not, I completely understand, and I'll get someone to tow your car to a lot."

Honestly, it's not as bad as I envisioned. The way he was acting in the kitchen made it seem like he totaled the thing. "Yeah, it's safe. I'm not going to rip you to shreds for hurting my baby."

Rather than coming all the way in, he pokes his head into the spacious room. "Are you sure?"

"Yes, I'm sure," I sigh. Men can be such babies when they think they've royally fucked up. "It's not terrible, just a small hiccup in getting it put back together again."

I run my fingers across the trunk, and Johnny's arms wrap around me. "Kind of like Humpty Dumpty."

"No. Not like him. The rhyme says he couldn't be put back together." I turn until I'm facing him, my arms going around his neck. "And you'll get her all fixed up and pretty again…or else."

He bends down, placing small kisses along my cheek. "Or else what? It's not like you're big enough to actually hurt me or anything."

A small smirk crosses my lips. "You remember what happened last night?" He nods and grins. "Yeah, that won't happen as frequently."

"Now you're playing dirty." His hand slides down my side until his fingers trace the bottom of my shirt. Well, his shirt. He lifts it, slowly, gliding his fingers across the bare skin of my legs. A part of me wants him to keep going. To pull the shirt off completely, and bend me over the car. But one look at said car shuts that feeling down pretty quickly. I miss my baby, and I need to be behind the wheel again.

"Nice try, Johnny." I back away from him, trying to get my breathing under control. "How about you work on my car, and I'll organize some work stuff while you do it." He scrunches up his nose, clearly not in favor of my suggestion. "I'll even sit out here with you."

"There are about a million other things I'd rather be doing," he mutters under his breath.

Yeah, me too, buddy. Me too.

I don't know why I thought I would get any work done sitting out here watching him fix my car. This asshat decided he was going to take off his shirt. It's almost as if he is punishing me for making him do it. He's the one who backed into a damn fence.

He stands up from under my hood, and I stare down at my phone so he doesn't think I have been ogling him this whole time. "Hey, are you hungry?"

"I could eat." In my rush to see what the hell was wrong with my car, I totally spaced on eating breakfast.

"I guess we better get dressed then." He grabs a black stained rag off one of the work tables, and wipes his hands off. It doesn't do much good because there are still streaks of what I'm assuming is oil covering his hands.

"Why?"

"Because, I told Angie we'd stop in the bar today."

I vaguely recall him talking to her before we left the bonfire. I was too focused on the unannounced guest that crashed the party to fully listen. "Oh, okay. Can we run by my house so I can get some clothes?" I don't want anyone to see me in the same smoke smelling clothes I wore last night.

"Sure." His strides are long as he walks toward me. "Why don't you run to your house, and I'll take a shower to get all this grease off of me. Then I'll pick you up, and we can head into town."

"Sounds like a plan." Truth be told, I feel like I need a shower, and it will be nice to be in clothes that are mine. Johnny found a t-shirt and some sweatpants for me to wear. The pants are baggy even after tightening them all the way and double knotting the string. I hop down from the table I'm sitting on, and Johnny steps back. I'm not taking any chances of him getting his hands on me. If that happens, there's almost zero chance we'll actually go get food, and my stomach is growling. "See you at my house in twenty?"

He groans and slides his hands over his face, leaving black streaks on his cheek. "Yeah, I'll see you then." I wasn't playing when I said that I wanted my car fixed. Although, I'm not sure how long I can resist him. At least not after last night. I had a taste of what it feels like to be with him and I am hooked.

Chapter Twenty-Three

AFTER A RIDICULOUSLY LONG drive we finally pull into Out of the Ashes. Okay, maybe I'm exaggerating just a bit, but when there's nothing to look at except cows and fields during the twenty-minute drive…it seems endless. If I go anywhere in Austin it can take just as long to get there, but there are so many other things going on that I don't even notice the time passing by. Unless, of course, I hit traffic. The only traffic people out here have are tractors going slow on the main road. It's weird, and something I never thought would happen to me, but I've gotten stuck behind those huge ass vehicles twice in the past week that I've been here.

"Are you going to sit there and stare out the window the whole time?"

"Huh?" I shake my head.

"Are you ready to go in or do you want to go back to my place?" He laughs.

Rolling my eyes, I reach for the door handle. "Someone is a little sure of themselves."

"What can I say?" He shrugs and opens his door. "For

all I know you were over there thinking about all the ways I can make you feel good, and want to head back home. How many times was it you said my name last night?"

"Whatever. Let's go eat, I'm starving."

The bar is relatively quiet considering its lunch time on a Saturday. I figured the place would be filled to the brim with college football playing on the few TV screens they have around the bar. I really need to set aside some time to talk to Angie, even if it means parking my ass in the bar stool while she works.

"Hey guys," Angie waves at us as we approach the bar. "Do y'all want to sit at a table or the bar? As you can see, you have your pick."

"Is the bar good with you?" Johnny whispers in my ear, sending shivers down my spine. Does he have to put his mouth so close to my skin? He knows what that does to me.

"Yep," I nod. "There's no use making her run around all over the place. We should make it easy for her."

"The bar is good, Ang."

He grabs my hand and pulls me toward the stools in the corner, as far away from the door as possible. "Why are we sitting way over here?"

"I don't like my back toward the door."

"That doesn't even make sense. Do you think some hitman is going to come in and take you out?"

His head whips back, and he stares at me for a few moments. "Your mind works in weird ways, Stella. I just like being able to see who's coming in and out."

"So, what you're saying is you're just as weird as me?"

"I guess."

"Do y'all want your usual?" Angie is wiping the counter down in front of us.

"Yep. Except can I have one of those beers you gave me last night?"

"I'm good with the same. Thanks, Angie."

"No problem. I'll go let the cook know what y'all want."

"You're the best," Johnny smiles.

Angie turns toward the kitchen and disappears behind the swinging door. "What were you working on this morning while I was killing myself getting your car put back together?" He still hasn't let go of my hand, and I'm not mad about it. It feels nice. Like our hands were meant to be intertwined.

Groaning, I lean my head against his shoulder. "The stuff for the Job Fair. I have no idea how I'm going to get it all done and set up by myself."

"You know it's okay to ask for help, right?"

"Yeah," I sigh. "I'm just not used to being the one that asks. Mr. Granger usually piles all of his work on me, and I'm the one that has to deal with it all while he takes credit for it."

"That sucks, and it's one of the reasons why I don't think I'll ever be able to work for a corporate company."

"I don't blame you. I love my job, I do, but sometimes I wonder if I'd be happier doing something else."

"Have you ever done anything else?"

"Nope," I pop the *p*. "I was hired by Mr. Hart as soon as I graduated from college. I worked my way up from grunt to assistant for one of the project managers. If I can get this center up and running without any problems, I'll be promoted to project manager myself."

He squeezes my hand, and the small action lets me know he's actually listening. "That's pretty impressive. Not many people stay at one job for very long."

I look up at him, his strong jawline in my view. I'm not sure that I've ever noticed another guy's jawline. "How long have you been a mechanic?"

"All my life," he smiles. "My grandpa taught me how to work on cars, and when my uncle needed someone in the shop full time after I graduated from high school, I went there."

"So, you've been there a while." It's a question, but not really. It's obvious it's the only place he's worked.

"Yep. The customers can be a pain in the ass sometimes, but I love what I do." He glances down at me, "It makes me happy."

He's so content with his life working at the shop. I don't think I've ever met anyone that is perfectly happy with their position and doesn't want more. It's refreshing. "I can tell. If only your happiness could lead you to finish fixing my car."

Johnny presses his lips together to hide a smile. "Truth be told, I've been taking my sweet time on your car. I could have had it fixed within two days."

"What?" I shriek.

Angie pokes her head through the door. "Is everything okay?"

"Yeah, sorry. I didn't mean to scare you."

"Calm down, Stella." He pulls my hand into his lap. "It's not because I'm lazy, or anything. I just knew that if I finished your car fast, then I'd never see you again."

"This town is tiny. There's no way we wouldn't have run into each other." The smell of our wings coming from the kitchen makes me sit up taller. We should have come sooner because right now I'm so hungry I might eat my napkin.

"True enough. But, I'm not sure that you would have agreed to go on a date with me."

"You knew the second you cornered me in the kitchen that I was going to say yes. I don't know what it is about you, but I don't think I could deny you anything."

His lips curl up. "Oh yeah. So, you wouldn't say no if I said we should get out of here and go back to my place."

"Well maybe not anything," I snort. "I'm on the edges of hangry and if I don't get food soon…it won't be pretty."

"Okay, okay." He holds up his hands in surrender. "So, what do you need help with for this Job Fair?"

It's more like what do I not need help with. "Honestly, everything. I have the tables, chairs, and snack trays ordered. I just don't know how I'm going to set it up and man everything on my own."

"Just give me the date and I'll help you."

His generosity has no bounds. "And what do you expect in return?"

"Nothing…" he shrugs. "Though, I wouldn't say no to a repeat of last night." There goes that devilish grin again.

Men. I roll my eyes, but I can't deny I am considering it. The people in this community know him, and trust him. "We'll talk about it. Your help would actually be great. It's during the week. Will you be able to get off work?"

"I have plenty of vacation time banked. Besides, my uncle wouldn't say no to me helping you."

"Then consider it a deal." His offer to help eases so much stress from my shoulders, and I visibly relax. That is until Angie comes out of the kitchen with our food. The plate has barely hit the bar top, and I'm picking up one of the wings to shove into my mouth. It must have just come off because it's so hot that it slips from my fingers, and slams back on the plate.

"Slow down and give it a second to cool off," Johnny laughs. "It's not going to go anywhere."

"Yeah, yeah. I'm not used to going this long without eating. I'm pretty sure my body is pissed at me right now."

"Suit yourself." He takes a sip of his beer and lets his food cool down while I dig in without abandon. It's a good thing I'm not one of those girls that will only eat a salad to appeal to men. What's better is that it doesn't seem to faze him how I am devouring these wings. Some of the guys I dated back in Austin would try to order for me. They obviously didn't know what to do with women that actually do things for themselves.

The grocery store selection in Asheville isn't very big. There are two chain stores and one local store. Even though I primarily eat fast food, I need to grab things I can snack on when I don't have time to go get something. Or, when I'm lying on the couch bored, and binge-watching TV shows. Of course, Johnny drives us to the smaller grocery store. Hopefully they have the type of stuff that I like. It's not like I'm difficult to please or anything. Just point me in the direction of all the crap food and we should be good to go.

"What do you want for dinner?" Johnny asks as he grabs a cart from beside the door.

"We literally just ate. How can you already be thinking of food again?"

The store is on the small side, but the multiple aisles of food eases some of my worry. I shouldn't have a problem finding the snacks I like. Newspaper clippings and photos of the high school football team plaster the walls when you walk in. It's a nice touch, and I can understand why Johnny brought me here instead of one of the bigger stores. This town thrives on community and the pictures show how much pride they have.

"Because I'm pretty sure we are going to have to eat again at some point today." He pushes the cart down the first aisle, searching for something.

"Good point." A box of fruit snacks catches my eye, and I grab it before throwing it in the cart. "The only problem is I don't cook. If it's not frozen, or take out, I don't eat it."

"You know that shit is bad for you, right?" Dammit, is he one of those people who get all judgy about others' food choice. Because if that's the case, this isn't going to work out. I don't need a man dictating what I can and can't do. The only person I allow to do that is Mr. Granger, and that's because he's one of the people responsible for my paycheck.

Shrugging my shoulders, I continue scanning the snacks that are on the shelf. Some of these I haven't had since I was a kid. Into the cart the boxes go. I have exactly zero cares to give what other people think about what I eat. "Yeah, I know that. But I also know that I can't cook, and that poses a problem when making healthier foods."

"It can't be that bad." He stares at me before he turns down the next aisle. "Haven't you ever made macaroni and cheese, or boiled eggs?"

"Yep, and they both turned out inedible." I glance away so he can't see my face. "I, um, let the water boil so long there was nothing left inside the pan."

"Well, today is your lucky day. I'm going to teach you how to cook."

"That really isn't necessary." I spy a bag of hot Cheetos

and throw it into the cart. If anybody saw the contents of the cart, they'd think a college kid was buying food for their dorm. "I can always run into town and pick us up some food."

We turn down yet another aisle, and he stops in front of jars of pasta sauce. "Nope. Spaghetti is easy enough. It's almost impossible to screw it up."

"You've clearly never met me before," I mutter under my breath.

"What was that?"

"Oh, nothing. Spaghetti sounds great." Little does he know that I have zero plans on helping him. I'm going to sit back and watch. A man that can cook is beyond sexy.

We're almost done getting everything we need for dinner tonight. The last stop is the produce area to pick up a few things for a salad. Johnny is too busy inspecting lettuce to see the woman making her way toward us. This shit seriously cannot be happening. Does she have some kind of homing beacon on him?

"Hi, Johnny." Sarah's voice is sugary sweet, but the daggers her eyes are shooting my way are anything but.

Johnny's back stiffens at the sound of her voice. He takes his time placing the lettuce in the cart before facing her. "Um, hi, Sarah." His voice is tight, and he reaches for my hand for moral support. "You remember Stella?" Nice subject change, buddy. Too bad it's as obvious as a two by four to the head.

Sarah scrunches up her nose in disgust. "Yes, how are you?"

Funny how she saw me and didn't acknowledge me, but one little question from Johnny and suddenly I appeared to her. "I'm fine." I refuse to ask her how she's doing. Call it bad manners, I don't care. She walked over here with an agenda to make me feel like shit, and I just can't let that stand. "We were actually just about to head out." The only way to get this woman to understand that she can't push me around is to put a stop to the conversation, and make an abrupt exit. Some may say that I'm being a coward, and I'm okay with that. These two have a history together and she still makes him uncomfortable after all of these years. Even though I have no idea exactly what we are to each other, I don't share. I'm not letting her worm her way back into Johnny's head. Tiffany would be so proud of me for standing up for what I want. I just wish I knew where all of these overprotective feelings have come from. I don't attach myself to others easily, and no other guy I have dated has pulled this sort of emotion out of me.

"Can I speak with you for moment, Johnny?" Geez, this girl does not get a hint. If he wanted to talk to her, he would.

"Actually, now isn't a good time." Johnny grabs the cart and starts walking away pulling me along with him since he still has a hold on my hand. "We have things we need to do."

"What are we doing?" I whisper to Johnny once we're a few feet away. If he thinks I'm doing anything strenuous, he's out of his mind. Though, there are a few things I still need to iron out with the Job Fair. And since he offered to help, it'll work out perfectly.

"Nothing. We're going to go to your house, relax, have an amazing dinner, and just hang out."

That actually sounds like a really fun night, and I push anything that has to do with the Job Fair out of my mind. Removing my hand from his, I wrap my arm around his waist. Walking side by side like this is awkward, but I'm doing it so Sarah can see that she's not going to wreck whatever it is that we have going on between us. I glance back, making sure she sees us. Her mouth is hanging open and her eyes are wide. If I'm not mistaken, her cheeks look pinker than they did before. Mission accomplished. I hope Sarah has this image burned into her head for the rest of the day.

Chapter Twenty-Four

THE PAST FEW weeks with Johnny have been amazing. We've spent more time together than we've spent apart. I'm either at his house or he's at mine. I've almost forgotten what it feels like to sleep alone. He makes me feel better than I've ever felt before. And the help he's given me with this Job Fair has been more than I could ask for.

He's unloading tables, while I grab all the paperwork I'll need for every station. Each one will cover a different job, and I hope we get a lot of applicants. I need every position filled before I can leave this town and go home. The thought sends a pang through my chest. What's supposed to happen when I leave? Will we continue the long-distance thing? Or, go our separate ways? We still haven't made anything official, but I can't stop these feelings from growing every moment we spend together.

I know that I shouldn't be hanging out with him as much as I have been, but I can't fight this pull I have toward him. I can leave work with all kinds of stress and pressure weighing on my shoulders, and the minute he wraps his arms around me all of the negativity melts away.

The guy who brought the tables is pulling out of the parking lot, and Johnny comes in to the small office. "How do you want these tables set up?"

"I have no idea. I feel like if we put them in rows potential employees will undoubtedly miss some of them." I tap my finger against my chin trying to figure out the best setup. "Maybe a U-shaped layout would be best. Then they can just hit one table after the other to see if they're interested in the position and fill out whatever paperwork I have on the table."

"That's a good idea." Johnny looks at the stack of vegetable trays on my desk. "What are we going to do with that stuff?"

"Just leave one table open in the middle and we will set it on there."

"You're the boss," he gives me mock salute and walks out into the warehouse area. He is such a smart ass. It's a good thing he's hot as hell. It's almost time to get this thing going.

I breathe a sigh of relief. So far there has been a steady flow of people. I was worried that nobody was going to show up, but Johnny assured me that there are a lot of people in this town willing to work. They just needed an opportunity to open up for them. Even though I dreaded relocating here, it really has turned out for the best.

There is only twenty minutes left of the Job Fair, and my feet are hating me. I should have worn flats, or anything besides these heels. I'm not used to actually standing in them. Almost everybody has left and I start cleaning up the abandoned tables. The boxes holding their personal information need to be sorted through, and I stack them all up on one table.

"Oh no, did I miss the fair?" And just like that, my happiness over the success of the event diminishes. What is she doing here?

Forcing a smile on my face, I turn around. "Hi, Sarah. We are just wrapping things up. How can I help you?"

"If you're already cleaning up, I can just submit my resume to your company directly." Excuse me, what? Did she just say what I think she said?

"Oh, I didn't realize you were in the market for a job." Please let this be a joke. I cannot be the person who has to interview this woman, let alone work with her.

She looks around the warehouse, squinting at the room. "I wasn't, but I've decided I'm going to stay here for a while."

My heart clenches, and I can't fathom a reason for her to stay in Asheville aside from Johnny. She'll be there to swoop in as soon as I'm gone. "Wh—what type of job are you looking for?"

"Something in management. No offense, but I'm not cut out to do grunt work." I hate that she refers to manual labor as grunt work. Everything about this woman rubs me the wrong way.

"Yeah I have those forms right over here." The table isn't very far away, but I don't want to turn my back to her. I have this feeling like she's up to something. However, we are both grown women, and our bitchiness toward each other is beyond childish. We don't have to like each other. Turning toward the table that has the management applications, I quickly walk to it and pick one up. "Here you go."

"Thank you. Do you have somewhere I can sit to fill this out?"

There's only one place she can have privacy to do it, and I'm not leaving her in the small office alone. "Let me grab you a chair, and you can sit at one of these tables to fill it out." She huffs as I rush to my temporary office to get her something to sit on. If there were other people here, I'd make her stand with a clipboard like everyone else did. But I just want her out of here as fast as possible.

Sarah is quietly filling out the application while I continue clearing the tables. The only sound coming from the cavernous room is the sound the pens make as they hit each other in a box. I jump when I hear a deep voice from somewhere behind me. "What are you doing here?" Johnny's voice is gruff.

"Applying for a job, silly." Sarah's voice is high and flirty, and I grit my teeth to keep from saying anything. The familiarity she has with him makes me crazy, and sad. I've never had that with anyone other than my cousins.

"I didn't realize you were here to stay."

"I haven't fully made my decision, but it's nice to have a plan if I decide to." That little liar. That is not the story she gave me before asking to fill out an application.

"And this is where you decided to apply?" Watching them speak to each other is like watching a ping-pong match and trying to figure out which side is going to win. I don't miss the skepticism in his voice, though. He fully believes she had ulterior motives coming here today, and that makes me feel a little less crazy about the whole thing.

"Well, I can't put all my eggs in one basket. This isn't the only place I'm applying."

I can't help but roll my eyes. This lady spouts off so much bullshit, and believes everyone is going to take her word for it. I know what attention seeking looks like. Tiffany could give a master class. Either way, I feel like I need to save Johnny right now. "Are you almost done filling out your application? I need to finish getting these tables taken down in time for the guys to come pick them up."

"Here you go." She places the application on the table I'm next to, gathers her things and walks toward the door. "Hopefully I hear from your company soon."

"Thanks." Hopefully that one word didn't come off too bitchy, but everything about her drives me insane. Not to mention she's trying really hard to get Johnny back, and that's just not going to happen. At least I hope not. She's turning this into a competition and I'm too old to be playing games like this. Johnny doesn't seem like he's falling for her crap, though.

Once Sarah is out of the building Johnny grabs my hand. "You aren't seriously going to turn the application in, are you?"

"Of course, I am." I pull my hand from his. How could he even think I wouldn't? "It would be unethical of me not to. My whole promotion at the company rides on this warehouse opening up without a hitch. If word got out that I didn't turn something in because I didn't like a person, it would be career suicide."

"Yeah. I get that. I'm sorry for even suggesting it." Johnny takes a step toward me and grabs my hand again. "I just know that everything she wrote on it is probably a lie, and she's doing all of this to get under your skin. I don't want her to hurt you."

"I appreciate your knight in shining armor routine, but

I'm a big girl. I can handle myself. You don't get as far as I have in my industry without having thick skin and a backbone. Besides, if she lied on any part of the application, the people in HR will figure it out."

He pulls me into him, chest to chest. "I have no doubt that you'll get the promotion. And I know you can take care of yourself. I know how she is, though. She's vindictive as hell and will do anything to get what she wants."

"You realize that will only work if that's what you want too, right?" Fear creeps up my spine at what he might say to that. We haven't established what we are, and whether I continue to date him or not hinges on what he says next.

"I don't want her. I haven't in a long time." I breathe a sigh of relief. "*You* are the only person I want." He runs his hand through my hair. "I want to be more than casual with you. God. I feel like a dumbass teenager even asking this, but what do you say to being my girlfriend?"

Holy shit. He wants to be a legit couple. Does that change anything? I mean, we're already doing things that couples do. This just makes it official.

"Stella? I'm not sure if I should take your silence as a yes or no."

"Yes," I scream and throw my arms around his neck. A little dramatic, maybe. But this man sets my soul on fire, and makes me feel like I can have it all. The career and the relationship.

Chapter Twenty-Five

"What is that noise?" Johnny groans from the other side of my bed.

"I don't hear anything. Go back to sleep." He must've been dreaming about something because there's not a single sound coming from my room.

"I swear I'm not going crazy. It sounded like something was vibrating." He pulls me closer to him and nuzzles my neck. "You aren't hiding any toys, are you?"

I push him away and laugh. "No, you perv." Actually, I do have some hidden away, but there has been no use for them. He gets the job done just fine. A buzzing sound comes from my dresser, and I sigh. It's early, and the only person who would be calling is my boss.

"Told you I wasn't crazy," Johnny mumbles. The phone stops vibrating, but whoever is calling is adamant because it starts right back up. "Would you answer it already? They obviously aren't going to stop calling, and that means we don't get to sleep in."

He has a point, but I'm not going to tell him that. "Fine," I huff. Reaching toward the nightstand, I grab my phone and answer it without looking at the screen. "Hello?"

"It's about damn time you answer your phone." Tiffany's voice startles me. Something has to be wrong because she never calls this early. "I thought we were going to have to send out a search party."

"I'm fine," I say. "Is everything okay over there?"

"Yup. We just haven't talked much, and I was worried something had happened." That's not normal for Tiffany. She usually checks in whenever she feels like it, or when she wants something. "How's the job going?"

Why is she acting so weird? "It's fine. I put on the Job Fair a couple of days ago, and we got a lot of applicants. Where's Audrey?"

"I'm here." It's good to know they still have each other even though I'm hours away. Not being with them stings, though. Normally we'd be seeing what trouble we could get into for the day. Now they are living their lives, and I'm settling into a routine without them.

I glance over at Johnny and grimace. Covering the phone receiver, I whisper, "This may take a while."

"I'll run into town and grab us some breakfast." He gives me a quick peck on the cheek. "Tacos sound good?" When I nod, he grabs his clothes and gets dressed. "I'll be right back."

"Was that the hot mechanic?" Now I've gotten Tiffany's attention. "Is it as good as you imagined?"

"Tiffany," I hear Audrey admonish her, then a dull thwack. Holy shit, I think Audrey just hit Tiffany. "You don't ask people things like that?"

"She's not people," Tiffany grumbles. "She's our Stella."

If I don't jump in, these two will argue for the next thirty minutes. "First off, he has a name. It's Johnny."

"Okay, then is Johnny better than you imagined?"

This girl will be the death of me. I roll my eyes, and answered her question anyway. "Not that it's any of your business, but yes." I can't stop the stupid smile that takes over my face. "He's amazing in so many ways."

"Uh oh," Tiffany sings songs. "It sounds like somebody's catching feelings."

"That's insane," Audrey butts in. "Stella isn't stupid enough to start something with a guy when she knows she's leaving soon. Right, Stella?"

"Well," I begin. But Audrey cuts me off.

"You're in a relationship with him?" She screeches. "That's probably one of the most irresponsible things you have ever done. What were you thinking?"

Geez, maybe she'll tell me how she really feels. Tiffany comes to my defense. "Hey, lay off of her. She sounds happy. Happier than she's sounded in a really long time, actually." It's odd that Tiff is the one that has my back. It's usually her against the two of us, but this time I'm grateful she's in my corner.

"Thanks, Tiff." I grab the pillow Johnny was using this morning and prop it up to block some of the sunlight. "I am happy. He makes the hard days seem better, and we have fun when we're together."

"What are you going to do when you come home?" Tiffany whispers, unknowingly breaking any joy that I'm feeling. She just had to ask the hard question.

"I'm not sure. I guess we'll see when it happens."

"Who is this girl that takes things day by day, and what did she do with my workaholic cousin?" Tiffany laughs.

"Just think of all the fun times we could have had with this version of you."

"Shut up," I groan. "I'm still the same me. Just a slightly less stressed version. Now I know what all the love sick girls in the RomComs we used to watch feel like."

"Has it gone that far?" Audrey questions.

"Gone that far for what?"

"You said love sick," she says. "Do you think it could be love?"

"I don't know," I whisper. It's something I haven't considered. I'm not even sure what love feels like since I've never been in love before. "What does it feel like?"

"Don't ask me," Tiffany snorts. "I've never once in my life claimed to love anyone. I keep them around until they are no longer fun."

"I wasn't asking you smartass. Audrey?" She has to be able to tell me. She was in a serious relationship when she was in high school. Though, she never said why it didn't work out.

"It kind of sounds like it," she finally answers. "If you can't imagine what it would be like without him, I'd say that's a pretty good indicator."

"Well, shit." It looks like I'm screwed when I leave because I'll be leaving my heart here. Maybe Audrey was right, and I've done something I shouldn't have. She *did* try to warn me before she headed back to Austin.

A door slams outside, and I sit up. Weird, I didn't hear Johnny's truck coming down the driveway. "Hey, I think Johnny may be back with food. I'll call y'all later."

"You better," Tiffany demands. "I have roommate drama I need to fill you in on."

"See," I laugh. "That's what you should have led with. Love y'all."

"Love you, too," they both scream in unison.

I hang up the phone and set it back on the nightstand. Johnny hasn't come inside, yet. At least not that I know of since the front door didn't make its usual creaking noise. I don't know who else would be coming by, though. I still don't know very many people here. Getting out of bed, I grab the robe I left on the floor last night. Hopefully it's someone that doesn't mind the just rolled out of bed look.

The stairs are cool against my bare feet as I make my way down to the kitchen. There's a bag from one of the mexican restaurants in town sitting on the counter, so he has to be back. Why didn't he come upstairs and get me? A better question is why didn't I hear him come in? "Johnny?" I call out. "Are you here?"

No answer. I'll just take a quick peek out the front door. If his truck isn't sitting in my driveway, then I'll freak out. I grab a knife from the drawer, in case something crazy is about to happen, and tiptoe toward the door. Cracking it open, I look in the driveway. Johnny's truck is nowhere in sight. As I close the door, something catches my eye.

No fucking way. *My car* is parked where his mom's car should be. I throw the door open, and run onto the porch. "Sweet baby Jesus," I scream into the quiet morning. "I've missed you so much." I drop the knife and almost trip down the stairs to get to my baby.

I'm so busy checking every nook and cranny on my car that I don't realize Johnny is actually here until he wraps his arms around me. "Are you surprised?"

"By the car, or you sneaking up on me?" I turn until I'm facing him. "She's really ready?"

"I wouldn't have brought it over here if it wasn't." He

gives me a peck on the tip of my nose. "I was trying to get back before you saw it."

"First off, my car is not an 'it'." I notice his truck is back in the driveway. "Second, I didn't even hear your behemoth truck."

"How did you not hear it?"

"I was too enamored by this beautiful piece of machinery." I lean against my car. "Until recently, she's never let me down. Not that it was her fault." Stupid animal running me into a ditch.

"I won't let you down, either." That may be the cheesiest thing I've ever heard, but from him it's adorable. "Have you eaten yet?"

"Nope. I thought I heard something outside and came to investigate." There's one thing that doesn't make any sense. "How did you get here so fast after I heard the noise? There wasn't enough time for you to go all the way home and come back."

He shrugs and grins. "My mom was waiting at the end of the driveway with my truck. We switched vehicles and she went home."

Holy shit. His mom was here? "Why didn't you invite her to come in so I could meet her?" That's something most guys would do, right? Unless, of course, he doesn't want to introduce us.

"Honestly, I thought you would still be in bed, or on the phone with your cousins. Besides, there's plenty of time for you to meet her." That time is slowly dwindling, though. Now that the applications are turned in, I won't be here much longer.

"Yeah, I guess you're right." Those are both solid reasons, but I would have gotten up for the woman who loaned me her car without knowing who I was. It is plain to see that Johnny gets his giving soul from her. He wouldn't let me pay for anything on the car. "Let's go eat. I'm starving."

He picks me up, waiting until my legs are wrapped around him before walking toward the house. "I know something I'm hungry for." He winks at me. We're halfway across the porch when he comes to a stop. "Why is there a knife out here?"

"My protection."

"From me?"

"I didn't know it was you at the time. Your truck was gone, and I heard noises. It's better to be prepared." I tighten my grip around his neck as he bends down to pick up the knife.

"I thought you were laying off the scary movies. You know, because this house is the perfect setup for one."

"It's a hard habit to break when I've watched them my entire life with my cousins. It helps me feel more connected to them when I miss them and they aren't answering their phones."

"If you say so." He opens the door with his partially free hand. He bypasses the kitchen and my stomach rumbles. He wasn't kidding about wanting me. "Don't worry. You can eat after."

"After what?" I bat my eyelashes, feigning innocence.

"Don't be a smartass." He walks into my room and plops me on the bed. I could definitely get used to this whole alpha male thing.

His fingers go to the sash holding my robe together, working furiously to get it untied so he can see all of me. He's almost got it done when my phone rings. "Ignore it," he grunts.

I do, but it rings almost as soon as it has stopped. "I

swear I'm going to murder my cousins." They seem to only call at the most inconvenient time.

Johnny glances at my still ringing phone, and his brows furrow in confusion. "Who is Satan?"

Shit this can't be good. "It's my boss."

"He's calling on a Saturday?"

"Only when something is fucked up."

"Apparently nobody wants me to get laid this morning," he mutters. Poor guy. First, my cousins wake us up. Now this?

I scramble across the bed and snatch the phone from the nightstand. "Hello?"

"Stella, you have a huge problem." Mr. Granger's voice is hard and gruff. Dammit, what could have possibly gone wrong in such a short amount of time?

Chapter Twenty-Six

My stomach drops. This can't be happening. There's so much I have to do now. I've almost completely tuned Mr. Granger out, but the words he says before hanging up destroy my hopes. "Get it fixed now, or you're fired."

Can he even do that? I know Mr. Granger is still my direct boss, but I assumed if there were any problems, or concerns, they'd come from Mr. Hart. I move the now silent phone away from my ear, and drop it onto the bed. I will not let this snafu be the end of my career. To be the end of everything I've busted my ass for.

Johnny is now in my line of sight, crouching down until his eyes meet mine. "Is everything okay?"

Wet, tears slide down my face. "No, everything is going up in smoke."

"What happened?" He grabs my hand and pulls me off the bed until I'm on the floor next to him. Wrapping his arms around me, he brings me in closer. "Whatever it is, I'll help you in any way I can."

"Thanks," I sniff. "But I have to do it on my own.

Apparently, the forms I sent in weren't the correct ones. And one of the bay doors isn't working."

"How is the door your fault?" I don't miss that he mentions nothing about the applications. That is one hundred percent my fault. I should have made sure I had the updated ones.

"No idea." I wipe my nose on my robe, and curl into Johnny. "I need to find the contact number for the company that installed it. That's the easy part. It'll be much harder wrangling everyone together to fill out the applications again."

"I can help you with it."

"No, you can't. It's confidential information, and I would get my ass handed to me if I let someone else handle it."

He's silent for a few moments, unsure of how he can help alleviate my stress. This is what I get for spending so much time with him. I should have been focusing on getting this new center started off with a bang. Instead, I'm drowning in my own pit of failure. This is what I get. Audrey was right. I need to execute my plans instead of getting sidetracked by a man. He may be a man who makes me feel like I can do anything, but I need to back off a bit. Hopefully he understands. I have my job to save.

Johnny's voice breaks into my thoughts. "Well, I'll take care of the door repair. If the company can't get out here quickly, I'll do it myself."

"Do you even know what you're doing when it comes to those things?"

He whips his head back, hurt from my question. "Of course. We have the same type of doors at the garage, and I'm the one who does the repairs there."

"Sorry," I grimace. "I didn't realize you had actual

experience with things like that." I feel like a bitch for questioning his knowledge. He works on cars for goodness sake. "I'll run up to the building tomorrow to get all the information."

I start to stand, but Johnny touches my arm, stopping me. "Stella, it's Saturday, and you haven't eaten yet. Let's go chow down on those tacos I brought, and we'll figure out what to do tomorrow."

"You don't understand. I need to get this taken care of now." I stand up all the way, and tie my robe closed. "If I don't, I'll be fired. That means no promotion. No job. All my hard work…"

Johnny gets off the floor and sits on the bed. "It's not a good idea to go rushing off. You need to figure out how to get everyone to come in and refill everything out. Otherwise you'll be running around like a chicken with your head cut off."

He has a point. I won't be able to get anything done if I don't have a clear and concise plan. I can't afford to lose this job. Austin isn't exactly the cheapest place to live, and I'm not about to room with either one of my nosy cousins. "You're right," I sigh. "Let's eat. Maybe food will help me think better."

I'm so close to being done with Operation Save My Ass. Johnny called the company that installed the door, and they came out right away. I guess it's a good thing I have a boyfriend that knows all the local companies. I'm not so sure they would have made fixing the door a priority if I would have called them. Maybe they would have, who knows. I'm just glad it's done.

Almost everyone who originally filled out applications have come by to do the correct ones. They were more than understanding, and told me it wasn't a big deal. I'm only waiting on a few more, including Sarah. Maybe she really is going to stick around. She called me back and said she'd come in this afternoon sometime. My stomach has been in knots since I got off the phone with her.

The silence surrounding me is pure bliss. It's going to be odd hearing other people in the building when the new hires come in to train. That's okay, though. It's one step closer to being able to go home. And, leaving Johnny. I'm not so sure that's what I want anymore. He's become a staple in my life, and I'm terrified to rip it out.

I'm typing up the potential employees and putting them into the system myself. I want to make sure it's all properly done this time around. I'm not a hundred percent sure, but I think Mr. Granger had something to do with sending me the wrong forms.

My phone rings and I hit enter before I mean to. Ugh, I'm going to have to go in and correct that one. "Dammit," I mutter. "Whoever this is, it better be important."

A picture of Tiffany from one of the music festivals we went to flashes across my screen. I really need to put my phone on do not disturb when I'm working, or with Johnny for that matter. My cousins have the worst timing. If I don't answer, she'll blow up my phone until I do. "Yes, dear cousin. How may I assist you today?"

"Have you always been such a smart ass?"

"Since the day you were born. What's up?"

"You never called me back over the weekend, and I still need to fill you in on the roommate drama."

Crap. I knew I was forgetting to do something. "I'm so

sorry, Tiff. Shit hit the fan over here and I've been in panic mode."

"Did something happen with you and Johnny?" She's actually concerned with what's going on in my life. I can't tell if it's genuine, or if it's to keep her mind off her own problems.

"No. It's work crap. But I got it handled for the most part, with Johnny's help."

"That's good." She pauses for a few seconds and I'm worried the call has been disconnected. "I meant what I said the other day. You seem happier. I don't know if it's him, or the small-town life, but it agrees with you."

I can tell she's sincere. For once she isn't only thinking of herself. Maybe my little cousin is finally growing up. "Thanks, Tiff. That means a lot. I have no clue what I'm going to do when it's time for me to leave." That date will be getting closer and closer after we officially hire some people. "So, what's up with your roommate situation?"

"Besides the fact that I should put you and Audrey in charge of finding me one? Everything. This guy needed a temporary place to stay, and I felt a good vibe about him. There wasn't anything giving me any weird signals. But he was a total creep. He'd wait outside the bathroom door when I was showering, and was always hovering around."

"Tiffany, please tell me he's not still there. And if he is, take your ass to my apartment and call the cops." This girl is going to end up on the news one day if she doesn't start making smarter choices.

"He's not. After the second day I told him to get his shit and get out. I also told the security guy downstairs not to let him back up."

Thank God for that. "You've got to be more careful."

She cuts me off before I say anything else. "I know. I've

got a bunch of interested people in my email for the open room. I'm going to forward them to you and Audrey. Y'all are going to make the decision for me. Just remember, I need someone who isn't going to be all in my personal space or get on my nerves."

"So, anyone who isn't female and won't take any attention away from you?"

"Exactly."

"I'll get to it as soon as I can." A knock on the outside of the office door pulls my attention away from Tiffany. Sarah is standing in the doorway. I wish she would have given me a specific time so I could have prepared for her arrival. "Hey, Tiff. I'll call you back later."

"Okay. Talk to you soon. Love you." She hangs up as soon as the words are out of her mouth.

"Hi, Sarah. Thanks for coming in on such short notice. I'm sorry for the inconvenience." I point to the chair in front of my desk. "Have a seat, and I'll grab the correct application."

"No rush," she waves the comment away. "I got out of my appointment earlier than expected.

She really doesn't have to share her schedule with me. I don't care. But I can't tell her that in a professional capacity. I pull the application from a tray and hand it to her across the desk. "Here you go."

She grabs a pen out of the cup on my desk and begins filling it out. "How much longer are you here?"

Why? So, you can swoop in and make Johnny feel better when I'm gone? That's not what I say, though. "Probably a few more weeks. Corporate should be making hiring decisions by the end of the week. Then it'll be a couple of weeks for training. After that, we'll have the grand opening." I don't know why I just told her all of that information except for the fact that she makes me nervous, even when she shouldn't. This is my domain, damn it.

"Are you and Johnny going to do the long-distance thing?" She glances at me and her eyes brighten as she waits for my answer.

"I don't think that's appropriate to discuss in this setting." That's it, Stella. Take the classy way out. Don't let her make you feel like shit.

"He's not going to pick up and move to the city with you. He's a small-town guy through and through. There is no way a woman he barely knows will make him change his mind." She sets the pen and application on my desk and leaves without another word. She's done what she came here to do, and it had nothing to do with the job she applied for.

What did I do to make her dislike me so much? She doesn't even know me, and she's been gunning for me since that night at Johnny's bonfire. She only wants what she obviously can't have, and instead of dealing with whatever emotions she has, she's made me the target.

I shouldn't let her get under my skin, I know that, but it doesn't stop me from texting Johnny.

Stella: What do you think about Austin?

A few minutes pass by with me staring at my phone, waiting for those three little dots to show up.

Johnny: I wouldn't mind visiting there.

Visiting, not going there to see you, or possibly moving there. He *knows* that's where I'm from. Without even realizing it, he's already sealed our fate.

Chapter Twenty-Seven

I'M NOT CUT out to train other people. The past two weeks have been brutal. It wouldn't be so hard if I actually knew how to do all the jobs' I'm showing these people. I've been relying on videos and printed material Rosie is sending me.

The biggest victory for me...Mr. Hart didn't do anything with Sarah's application. I debated even turning it in, but didn't want to stoop to her level. Maybe I'm a masochist, but I'm not one of those women that will keep another woman from excelling just because she's a thorn in my side. Now I only have to worry about her interfering in my life outside of work hours. If the cards are on my side, it won't be an issue even then.

An email from Mr. Hart comes through on my phone listing out the details of what is going to happen next. Apparently, he wants me to come back to the office for a couple of days next week to plan the ribbon cutting. It will be my first time going back home since I came to Asheville, and I'm nervous.

My phone pings with a message, and I close out of my email.

Johnny: Want to meet at Angie's place for dinner?

I only have a couple of days until I have to head to Austin. Going to dinner at a crowded bar isn't exactly how I want to spend time with him. But I can't be mad at him for suggesting it. He doesn't know about the travel plans that just got thrown at me. I mean, I assumed I'd have to go back before finishing things up here, but I didn't think it'd be so last minute.

Stella: That's fine. I can meet you there as soon as I make sure everyone else is out of the building. And, I have to head to Austin on Sunday.
Johnny: For good?
Stella: Not yet. They need me there to go over the details of the grand opening.
Johnny: Then I guess we better make tonight extra special.

Even though I don't want to go to Out of the Ashes, I'm excited to see Johnny. With me training, and him busy at work, we haven't seen each other as much as we were. And I'm not going to lie, I've been putting a little bit of distance between us since that text message. I probably should have talked to him about it when I got home that night, but I didn't want him to think that I let Sarah get into my head. All I know is that it's going to suck sleeping alone while I'm gone. Having him beside me at night is one of my favorite parts of the day. I'm so screwed.

The last few people in the warehouse finally walk out the door. Today is one of those days that feels like it's never going to end. I'm not sure if that's because it's Friday, or because I would much rather be wrapped up in Johnny's arms. Either way, I'm happy I can finally leave.

I lock up the building, and walk to my car. The weather is cooling off, and I wish I had brought a light jacket with me to work. It's crazy to me that I've been here for a season change. It feels like it hasn't been very long at all.

Unlocking my car, I slide into the driver's seat and pull out my phone.

Stella: I'm on my way.
Johnny: See you in a bit.

Out of the Ashes isn't very far from work which is why we meet there so often. The amazing wings are a bonus. Angie is at the bar training a new bartender when I walk in. "Hey Angie," I wave to her. "Have you seen Johnny?"

She nods her head toward the adjoining room. "He's at the table you usually sit at."

"Thanks. And, good luck." I point toward her trainee.

She rolls her eyes and then grabs a towel to clean up the mess her new bartender has just made.

I round the corner to the next room and stop in my tracks. Johnny is there all right. But Sarah has her arms around him. I can't believe what I'm seeing. He knew I was coming. Why in the hell would he let her hang all over him like that? Much less let her do it in public when we've made it known that we're an item.

Everything she said two weeks ago floats through my

head, and I can't stop the tears from sliding down my face. She was right. I've been falling in love with him, and he's just been using me. That's what I get for starting out on this journey with him. I should have kept it light and fun, or said no to begin with.

He still hasn't seen me. If I leave now, I can text him and say I'm not feeling well and decided to go home instead. That's a totally plausible excuse to not show up. Now to see if he buys it.

Pulling out my phone, I debate whether to send the text now or once I'm safely in my car, and away from the scene. It's probably best if I wait. I shove the phone into my pocket, take a step back, and turn to go right back out the front door. My only miscalculation is the waiter with a tray full of food in his hand. The tray clatters to the floor, and the chatter in the bar dies. This may be the only time I've heard the bar this quiet. So much for my quick escape.

Johnny's head pops up and his eyes meet mine. I can see the regret pouring out of his stare willing me to give him a chance. Sarah, however, is beaming. This is exactly what she wanted. For all I know she planned this little stunt, and was biding her time until she knew I would be here. My head says it's the most logical answer. But my heart only sees betrayal and pain. Johnny pushes her away and tries to stand up to get around her.

I don't wait to see what happens next. I rush through the front of the bar and out the door. My name from Johnny's lips is the last thing I hear before I'm enveloped by the chilly autumn air. I take a deep breath, and almost choke from the temperature change. The sobs trying to break free. I'm such a fucking idiot. I should have known better.

It's a good thing my car is parked close. My vision is

blurry from the tears, and there's no way I would be able to find my car in the back of the lot before he caught up to me. I get in and pull out of the parking spot. Looking in my rearview mirror, I see Johnny run out of the bar. I can take a right and go home. Or, I can take a left and hit the highway.

He's running toward my car now, but I can't face him. Not tonight. I need to get away from all these emotions. Away from Asheville. And, away from *him*.

I turn left. To my real home where the only things that matter are my cousins and my job.

My eyes are red and swollen by the time I pull into the parking garage at Audrey's apartment building. I could have gone to my own place. I should have. But I don't want to be alone. Not tonight. If I had my way, I'd undo everything that happened tonight and tell Johnny I'd rather stay in and cook dinner. Anything to keep *her* hands off of him.

There's a spot open next to Audrey's car, and I pull in. The drive here was exhausting. I didn't even stop to go to the bathroom. My cousins would be so proud of me. Maybe I'll just stay in the car. The thought of getting out and walking up fifteen million stairs to her apartment is already exhausting me. At least I'll get my cardio in.

The TV is loud as hell when I let myself in. She's about to regret giving me a key. I never show up unannounced. Hell, I didn't even call to let them know I was coming tonight. It was a split-second decision, and I fought back tears the entire drive here. A scream from the surround sound penetrates the otherwise quiet apartment. Shit, I hope I'm not interrupting a date. Talk about awkward.

I tiptoe into the living room to scope it out. Despite my own heartache, I don't want to interrupt whatever my cousin has going on. I prepare myself to see Audrey cuddled up with some hunky guy, but stop in my tracks when I see *both* of my cousins partially hiding behind a blanket watching one of my favorite horror movies. "You, assholes are watching *Halloween* without me?"

They scream and jump off the couch. "What the hell? You scared the shit out of us." Audrey bends down and picks up the popcorn that flew all over the floor when she jumped.

"Why didn't you tell us you were coming?" Tiffany asks. "We would have waited until you got here."

"I didn't mean to scare the pants off y'all." I drop my purse on the end table and help Audrey pick up the popcorn. "It was kind of last minute."

"How is kind of last minute an explanation? You live four hours away." Tiffany pulls the blanket they were sharing around her, and taps her foot. Waiting for me to answer her. Do I lie, or tell them the truth? I'm not in the mood for "I told you so."

"I was planning on coming home Sunday because they need me in the office on Monday, but..." I'm such a coward. I can't even finish the damn sentence. I stop my efforts in cleaning up the mess, and sprawl out on the floor.

Both of them look at me then search around for my bags. When they don't see any, Tiffany rushes to my side, wrapping her arms around me. "What happened?"

The tears I held back for over four hours run freely

down my cheeks. I can't stop them. As if the dam I had built up has broken. "His ex-girlfriend happened."

"Wait," Audrey holds her hand up. "He has an ex-girlfriend."

"Yes."

"And she's been giving you trouble?"

"I wouldn't say trouble, but she definitely hasn't been making my relationship with Johnny easy."

"Why didn't you tell us?" Tiffany pulls back. "We could have made a trip for moral support."

"Because," I sigh. "I'm a big girl, and I was handling it."

"What did she do to make you drive so far to get away from them?"

Rehashing the events that took place is frustrating, and I feel like a dumbass after I've told them everything. From the bonfire to the grocery store run in. And end with her applying for a job at the distribution center and what I witnessed before running to my car and driving here.

"That is such a classic bitch move," Tiffany wrinkles her nose in disgust. "I would know, I've done it."

"Um, Tiff," Audrey nudges her shoulder. "I don't think that's going to win you any favors right now."

"It's fine. I'm the idiot that let her get under my skin." I grab my purse off the table, and rummage through it for my phone. It's dead, of course. Charging it didn't even cross my mind when I got on the highway.

"You're not an idiot," Audrey rubs my back, and takes my phone out of my hand. "I'll charge it and give it back to you in the morning. Texting him right now isn't very smart."

"You're right." I grab the blanket from around Tiffany,

and climb up onto the sofa. "I think I'm going to try to get some sleep now."

Audrey and Tiffany wait until I'm lying down and tuck me in the way our moms used to do when we were kids and stayed with each other over the holidays. It's the little things that make you appreciate those in your life. "I love you guys," I mumble into the pillow.

"We love you, too." They turn the TV off and walk toward the kitchen whispering to each other just low enough so I can't make out what they are saying. It probably has to do with what a mess I've let myself become over a man. That's a turn of events I never saw coming.

Just before I fall into a deep sleep, I hear Tiffany talking. "She's asleep right now. Audrey and I are going to try to talk some sense into her over the weekend." I'll have to ask her about it tomorrow. Right now, I need to pass out so my brain will stop trying to overthink everything.

Chapter Twenty-Eight

"Okay, Stella," Audrey pulls the blanket off of me. "I love you, but you haven't moved from the sofa unless it was to use the bathroom since you got here Friday night. You have to go to work tomorrow, and you smell like death."

"No, I don't," I argue. Raising my arm, I take a sniff and scrunch up my nose. Maybe she's right about that. "Besides, it's not like I'm trying to impress anyone at work."

"Wrong," she points a finger in my face. "You still have to impress your bosses. You don't have that precious promotion yet."

Of course. She has to throw logic in my face like it's fucking confetti. I don't want any of it. I want to sit here and mope about Johnny. "Can I have my phone back?" They said they were going to give it back yesterday, but haven't done it. I don't understand why they are keeping it from me.

"Nope." Next she grabs the pillow I stole off her bed. The pretty ones on the sofa look comfortable but they are hard as hell, and my neck was not amused with me. "You are going to get your ass up, take a shower, and put on some of my clothes."

"Why?"

"Because it's Sunday, dummy."

"And?"

"We're having brunch. Tiffany should be here soon." Seriously...my love life is in turmoil and all they can think about is our weekly ritual.

"I'd rather sleep."

"Too. Damn. Bad." Audrey grabs my arm and pulls me off the couch. "Get up and get in the shower. Don't make me call your mom."

What the actual hell? "That's probably the most childish thing you've ever said."

"Well, you're acting like one." She starts walking to her bedroom. "If you aren't in the shower by the time I finish my makeup, I'm coming back with a cup of ice cold water."

This is the problem with being so close to my cousins. They know everything I dislike and they aren't afraid to piss me off. Why couldn't I have normal friends that won't give me the tough love treatment? Instead I'm stuck with these two crazies. Who am I kidding? I wouldn't have it any other way.

The apartment is silent as I walk out of the bathroom. Audrey was right, I *was* starting to smell. It's amazing what a shower will do for your attitude. The water washes the sadness away, leaving me feeling better. Not that I'm completely happy all of a sudden, but I feel fresh.

Like I can tackle this hurdle and still come out on top. Maybe?

"Audrey?" These two better not have left me here after making a big deal about getting off the sofa. She's not in the kitchen or living room. I open her bedroom door, and she's applying her lipstick. "Where's Tiffany?"

"She's going to meet us there." She rubs her pale pink lips together and glances at me. "We're taking your car, though."

This is weird. We always Uber to brunch, and we almost always go together. Something is going on, and I need to find out what it is. "Fine. But you're driving." I grab a hair tie off her dresser and put my hair up into a messy bun without bothering to brush it first. They'll take me how I am, or they can kiss my ass. "Are you ready?"

Eyeing me up and down, she nods. She grabs something out of one of her drawers then sweeps by me without a word. Is that my cell phone? I try to make a grab for it, but she drops it in her purse as she picks up my keys. "Let's go. With any luck Tiffany will already have a table for us by the time we get there."

The drive to the restaurant is boring. Audrey puts the radio on some talk radio station and doesn't say a word to me. I watch the cars pass by, and stare at the tall buildings as we drive through downtown. This used to be my normal, but now it doesn't hold the same feeling it once did. I can't help but long for the small town I've come to like. The nonexistent traffic in Asheville is pretty nice, too. It takes me less time to get from my house there to town than it takes us to get five miles from Audrey's apartment. Being here today is a good thing. I can acclimate to my world once again, and get back in the groove of things.

Tiffany is sitting at one of the front tables when we

walk in. Instead of her customary bloody mary in front of her, there's a glass of water. Audrey takes the chair next to Tiff, leaving me to sit opposite of them. "What is this? An intervention?"

"Sort of," Tiffany shrugs. "We need to talk about your priorities."

"Are you sure you should be leading this discussion?" Tiffany winces but doesn't show any sign of backing down. I'm already on edge, and I don't need these two trying to parent me. "I'm fine, guys. I'll be back here for good in a week, two tops."

"We don't think you should come back." Tiff's voice is barely above a whisper as she sneaks a look at Audrey.

"Wh-what?" She's kidding, right? There's no way I heard her correctly. "What do you mean I shouldn't come back?" The chatter of the restaurant seems louder than it was only seconds ago. Going from minor background noise to a constant buzzing. "Are y'all done with me, too?"

"Don't be stupid," Audrey scolds. "We'll never be done with you."

"Then why?"

"Because," Tiff raises her voice causing the couple at the table next to us to stare at her. "When you were in Asheville, you focused on you and what made you happy. It wasn't all about the job. You even met a great guy."

I can't believe this. "You agree with her?" I point at Audrey. "You thought dating Johnny was a mistake from the very beginning."

"Would you believe me if I said I had a change of heart?"

"No," I yell, not caring if I make a scene. "You don't get to stay on my ass about it then change your damn mind." I stand up and the chair falls to the floor. "After all the whining y'all did about me moving for my job, and you want me to *stay* there. Knowing damn well I don't have a reason to stay anymore."

I need to get out of here. Dozens of eyes are focused on me, and I stiffen. I'm making an ass of myself in one of my favorite places in Austin. I can't believe this. These two are something else. They are supposed to have my back. I was falling for Johnny. I can't go back there and see him all cuddled up next to Sarah. The pain would be too much.

Nope. I can't do this. Not right now when the pain is still too fresh. I grab my keys from the table where Audrey laid them down. "Y'all can have your weekly brunch. I'm out of here."

This feels like deja vu. Running out of yet another one of my favorite places to eat and away from the people I love. I can't believe they have the audacity to lecture me on my life. Even if they have a point, I can't tell them that. I've spent so much of my time and energy on trying to make it to the next ladder rung and I'll be damned if letting a man into my heart….

Tears blur my vision as I make my way toward the back of the parking lot. I look over my shoulder but my cousins aren't following me. Maybe they really are done with me. Finally, I get in my car, turn it on and start driving. The only place left for me to go is home, and I don't really want to be alone. I have work tomorrow, though, and I need to be ready for whatever they need me to do.

Once I'm safely inside my apartment building, I dig through my small bag for my phone. Shit. Audrey still has it. I hope to God that nobody from the office is trying to call me. It'll be the first time in a long time that I'll be unavailable.

The elevator is taking forever. I don't have time for this crap. I need to see what I have in my closet that I can wear, and figure out what I'm doing with my life. I slide the key into the doorknob of my apartment, twist it, and throw the door open. I'm back to a space in my life that is normal. This should be able to perk me back up, if not, I'm completely screwed.

With the door closed and locked behind me, I realize that I'm not alone. Audrey and Tiffany couldn't have beat me here. I slowly turn around and see *him*. "What are you doing here?"

I'm going to murder my cousins for this little stunt.

Chapter Twenty-Nine

JOHNNY DOESN'T SAY ANYTHING. He holds up his hands in surrender. This wasn't what I was expecting when I walked through my apartment door. "Seriously, why are you here?"

"You didn't give me a chance to explain before you ran out of the bar."

What the hell? Today is full of confrontations that I am not ready, nor am I equipped to handle. "I can't do this right now."

I turn back toward the door and lift my hand to the lock. "Dammit, Stella." Not once has he ever raised his voice at me. A part of me wants to walk right out the door and not look back. The other part, the one full of feelings and hope, thinks maybe I should listen to him. "Just, let me tell you what happened. Then, if you never want to see me again, I will walk out of your life and never bother you again."

Holy crap. He is being sincere. Normally he wraps his kindness in innuendo and dirty jokes, but I've never heard him this heartfelt.

I step away from the door, and walk to the living room, giving him a wide berth before I sit down on my sofa. God, I've missed this thing. It's much more comfortable than the crappy one Audrey has. I should have just come home Friday night instead of storming my cousins' apartment. I would have slept better at least. "I'll listen, but first you have to tell me how you even got in here." I have an idea; I only need confirmation.

He runs his hand through his hair and his cheeks redden. It's hard to stay mad at him when he looks so adorably uncomfortable, but I'm not going to let him off that easily. There's no reason Sarah should have been anywhere near him Friday night. "Your cousin may have let me in."

"I'm going to assume you're talking about Tiffany. When did you get here?"

"Yup. However, it also came with a threat to my manhood should I piss you off even more." He takes a step closer to me and stops when I hold up my hand. "I got here late last night. I couldn't leave my uncle hanging, so I worked all day. Then I got in my truck, and drove here. I needed to see you."

A man guilty of cheating wouldn't drive four hours to make his case, right? I've never had a serious relationship. Hell, I've barely had any one-night stands. There's no bar for me to measure this against. I have no idea what to think. This is where I need my cousins, even though I'm pissed at them. Maybe I imagined what I saw. Except all I keep seeing in my head is Johnny staring down at his phone, and Sarah pressed up against him. I shake the image away, "Now would be a good time to explain." Before I get mad all over again and start crying.

"First off, I don't blame you for running." Johnny takes

a deep breath and slowly lets it out. "And it wasn't at all what it looked like. I was sitting at the table checking my phone, and waiting for you to get there."

"So, how does Sarah fit into all this?" I interrupt him.

"If you would give me a second, I'm getting there." He watches me, waiting to see if I'm going to say anything else. When I don't, he continues. "I heard you talking to Angie, and I was about to send you a text letting you know where I was. Sarah, who I didn't even know was there, came out of nowhere and threw her arms around me at the same time you walked around the corner."

Although his explanation could be true, it seems a little convenient. "Why didn't you push her off of you as soon as she was touching you?" I'm not a jealous person, and I never have been. But, I'm not a fan of other people touching my things.

"I don't know. Because I'm not an asshole." He throws his hands in the air, exasperated. "I didn't want to have to physically put my hands on her. She can be vindictive when she doesn't get her way, as you might've noticed." Obviously. "I was trying to be civil since we were in public. But when I heard the tray hit the floor, and saw you standing there mortified, I had no other choice than to physically remove her from beside me."

He takes one, two, three steps toward me and crouches down until my eyes meet his. "Do you want to know why I would risk the possibility of her calling the cops on me for some bullshit reason?"

I can't say anything. It's like my brain forgot how to make words, and I shake my head waiting for him to continue. "Because of you. I don't give a shit about her, and I haven't for a long time. *You* are the one I want. You are the one I'm falling in love with. Hell, I think I partially fell in love with you the first night I met you and you accused me of being a serial killer."

I can't help the snort of laughter that bubbles from me. Only he would find my serial killer comments endearing. "Really?" It's a stupid question. I know it is as soon as it leaves my mouth. No guy in their right mind would drive this far for a girl they don't care about.

"Yes, really. I wouldn't have said it if I didn't mean it." That's one thing I've always been able to count on with him. He may be playful most of the time, but he doesn't sugarcoat anything. "Why would you think for one second that I was interested in Sarah?" I don't say anything. "I thought I made it pretty damn clear that I want nothing to do with her since the day she came back to town."

Because I'm a dumbass, that's why. "She may have made a few comments when she came to fill out the application again."

"What did she say?" He climbs up on the sofa next to me, and turns me until I'm facing him.

"Basically, that we'd never work once I moved back here." He looks like he's about to interrupt so I rush on. "And that you'd never pick up and move for someone you barely know."

He taps his finger on my leg, thinking. "Is that what the vague text asking what I thought about Austin was for?"

"Yeah," I squeak. I should have talked to him about it. But no, I let fear and her words dig into me so far that I couldn't let them go.

"That's not true. You know that, right?" I shrug because I don't. We never talked about the logistics of how we would work so far away from each other. "We can do the long-distance thing until we're ready to move forward. It wouldn't be hard for me to find a job here."

I don't want him to have to move for me, though. I'm not even sure I want to live here anymore. The noise and crowded streets aren't comforting the way they used to be. I miss the quiet of my house in the country. "I'm not going to ask you to do that."

"Just know that I would. The past two nights have been brutal not knowing what is going to happen to us." He leans forward and kisses me on the forehead before pulling me to him.

This feels right. It feels like home. "I'm sorry I ran away instead of talking to you. If I stayed, all of this could have been avoided."

"We're good now, aren't we?" I nod into his chest and his hold on me tightens. "Any chance your cousins are still at the restaurant? I'm starving and you have no food in the fridge."

"Yeah." I scoot back and scrunch my nose. "How did you know we were at a restaurant?"

"They texted me and told me where you'd be. They also said you'd probably get pissed and storm off." He pokes me in my side. "Is that something I'm going to have to get used to? You running off anytime I piss you off?"

I straighten my back. "Not unless it's something I really care about."

"It's nice to know you think I'm important," he winks at me, and tries to pull me toward him.

I resist. I may forgive him, but he's not going to goad me into giving him compliments. "Whatever. Let's go back to the restaurant." My stomach growls driving that point home. I haven't eaten actual food since Friday at lunch. It's a wonder my body hasn't gone into shock from all the ice cream and chips.

Johnny glances down the hall toward my bedroom and raises his eyebrows. "Do we have to go right this second?"

Smacking his arm, I stand up. "Yes, unless you want me to starve. There will be plenty of time for that later."

"I guess." He pouts.

"There will be." I grab his hand and pull him toward the door. "Until then, let me show you a little bit of my city."

At least it will be for now.

Chapter Thirty

WAKING up next to Johnny is the best I've felt since before my freak-out on Friday. I silence the alarm on my phone before it blares through the room. Apparently, it's annoying to him, or that is what I am guessing because he keeps hinting for me to change it to something less jarring.

As much as it pains me, I have to go into the office today. I have no idea what is going to happen once I get there. I've worked so hard to get this promotion, but it's not what I really want anymore. In a few short months, I have fallen in love with a man who changed everything. It's still weird admitting that I love him because I never saw myself settling down with someone, at least not for a few more years. But life is funny that way and takes you completely by surprise.

Lifting the comforter off of me, I attempt to slide out of the bed, but a muscular arm wraps around my waist and pulls me back. "Don't leave yet."

"Technically, I'm not actually leaving," I laugh. "I have to get ready." I untangle myself from his embrace and hurry out of the bed before he lures me back in. "Will you be here when I get back?"

"Probably," he mumbles into the pillow. "I don't plan on leaving until tomorrow at the latest. I already cleared it with my uncle."

"Good." I bend down and give him a quick kiss. I haven't told him that I plan on leaving with him. I just came to the conclusion myself. The only thing I know for sure is that being alone in this apartment is not what I want for my future, and I can't ask him to move away from everything he knows. He belongs in the country with me by his side.

My legs are shaky as I walk into the building. This was supposed to be a final planning meeting to sure up the distribution center and tell me my future within the company. Now, it's going to be a lot more than that. Hopefully, they will accept what I have to offer, but if not, I have a plan, thanks to Angie.

The elevator doors are almost closed when an arm coming through the crack forces them to open again. *He* is not the first person I wanted to see this morning. "Good morning, Stella. Are you ready for today?"

"Hi, Mr. Granger." I paste a fake smile on my face. Being in his presence grates on my nerves, but hopefully I won't have to deal with him for much longer. "Yes. I'm already."

"Good, good." He smooths his suit jacket and presses the button for our floor. I don't trust his smug smile. He's up to something, and even though I want to know what it is, I'm not going to bother trying to pry it out of him.

The elevator doors open and Mr. Granger turns right to go to his office. *Good riddance.* Instead of going to my office, I walk to the back of the room and turn for Rosie's desk. She's sitting in her chair painting her fingernails. She's such a rockstar and gives no fucks what others think. It's a good thing Mr. Hart likes her, or she would have been fired long ago. "Good morning, Rosie. How are you this fine morning?"

"Hi, Stella," she beams. "I'm good. Are you looking for Mr. Hart?"

"Yes, ma'am."

"He's in his office." She points a shiny red nail toward his office.

"Thank you." I take a deep breath and put one foot in front of the other. Each step taking me closer to either the biggest mistake I've ever made, or the beginning of a new adventure.

I knock three times in quick succession. "Come in," Mr. Hart calls through the thick wood. He's not at his usual place behind the desk. He's standing next to the tall window, staring out at the city.

"Good morning, Mr. Hart." He jumps at the sound of my voice, even though he told me to come in. "Sorry, I didn't mean to startle you."

"You're fine, Stella. How are you?"

"I'm great." And for the first time, in a long time, I mean it. Happiness fills every part of my soul, and I realize now that all I felt before was content. I was okay with only having work to fill my days, and it filled my nights a lot of the time, too. Now, I spend my time with a great guy and new friends.

"That's good." He walks around the desk and sits in one of the chairs in front of it instead of the big, leather one behind it. "You're here awfully early. Is there something you wanted to discuss before the meeting?"

It's remarkable how perceptive he is. I guess that's why most of his employees are happy and we don't have a ton of turnover when it comes to staffing. "Actually, yes."

"Why do I get the feeling that I won't like what you have to say?"

I don't beat around the bush; I jump right in with what I have to say. "Is the manager position at the distribution center set in stone?"

"Yes. Why?"

"Are there any other positions I could apply for?"

He sighs, "You know better than anyone that there aren't. *You* were the one in charge of training after we filled all the positions."

"That's what I figured." Deep breath in, long exhale out. Just say it. Don't hold back. I reach into my bag and pull out the letter I secretly typed up this morning. "I'd like to hand in my resignation notice."

His eyes widen. He wasn't expecting that. "Is there anything I can do to change your mind? Or, is there something we did as a company to push you away?"

"No, sir," I smile. "It's been amazing working here. It's just time for me to move on to something, and somewhere, else."

I hear a gasp come from the door I didn't shut all the way. Rosie is so nosy, and I can't stop my laugh. Mr. Hart glances at the door and rolls his eyes. "You might as well come all the way in, Rosie. There's no use hovering outside."

She claps her hands together without letting her fingers touch. That polish still has to dry after all. "You met someone, didn't you?"

Nodding my head, I look out the window at the city I'm going to leave behind. Not for good. I still have to come back and see my cousins, after all. "Not that it's any of your concern, but yes."

"Oh sweetie, I'm happy you finally found someone you're willing to stop working nonstop for."

"That's kind of mean. I dated."

"Not enough." She laughs at my scowl. "Don't think I didn't notice all of those late nights you spent up here. A young woman your age should be out enjoying life, not shutting herself up inside four walls."

She has a point. I didn't realize how much I was working until I was given the chance to slow things down. I'm not telling her that, though. She loves being right, and I won't give her the satisfaction. Instead, I change the subject. "I'll stay on until the grand opening, and however long you need me until you find a replacement. But I won't be able to come into the office as much."

"As much as it pains me to lose such an amazing employee, I'm fine with you staying until the opening." He stands up, and I do the same. "I'm not happy about this turn of events, but as long as you're doing what you think is best for you, I'll accept it." He holds his hand out, waiting for me to shake his. After I place my hand in his, he squeezes it slightly. From anyone else it would weird me out, but he's more of a grandpa figure in the office. "You're still getting that bonus, though. You've done an excellent job in handling everything with this new operation. You are going to make someone else a great employee."

"Thank you, sir." As much as I fight it, tears well up in my eyes. It's a bittersweet ending my journey with the company, but it's for the best. It's time to move on to bigger and better things.

Johnny is sitting on the couch scrolling through my saved Netflix shows when I get home. It's a total mix-up of different genres, and he's probably worried about the kind of girl he's dating. It's too late now. He's stuck with me. "How was work?" He pauses his scrolling, and pats the space next to him on the sofa.

"It was…good." I grin from ear to ear. Mr. Granger tried his best to prove what an inept person I am, and why I don't deserve the promotion. It was satisfying watching his face fall when I announced my resignation. He's only mad because he wasn't the one that pushed me out the door.

"When is the grand opening?"

"Next week. There isn't much left for me to do to finish up the project. The PR team is getting the local paper to write a piece about the opening and get some pictures. All I have to do is show up and cut a ribbon."

"Oh," his face falls. "I guess that means you'll be here permanently after that."

I shrug my shoulders, making him wait for my news. It's cruel, but he'll be happy about it in the end. "Are you ready to go home?"

"Damn, you're already kicking me out?" He laughs in an attempt to disguise the hurt.

"No, weirdo," I shake my head. "With me."

"You're already home." He stares at me in disbelief.

"To Asheville." It's like I have to spell it out for him. It's still not registering. "Home is where you are."

"Does that mean what I think it means?" His eyes brighten and he pulls me into his lap.

"Yes, it does." I kiss him on both cheeks and grab his face between my hands. "I'm moving to Asheville…permanently."

"That's the best damn news I've heard all day." He looks around the apartment. "You've got a nice set up here, but it's nothing like the fresh country air."

"How about we say goodbye to my apartment properly before we leave in the morning?" I climb off his lap, grab his hand and pull him off the sofa.

"I lied," he grins. "That's the best news I've heard." He sweeps me in his arms and carries me to my bed.

I never thought I'd find a reason to leave the city. But here he is. He helped me see there's more than just working day in and day out. I am ready for the next chapter in my life, and I think the slow and steady pace of Asheville suits me just fine.

Epilogue

Food covers the counters of my kitchen. Johnny's friends from work, Angie, and my cousins are in the living room while we try to figure out the best placement for everything. Friendsgiving is something I've always done with Audrey and Tiffany before we'd get together with our entire family.

"Where do you want the turkey?" Johnny asks from behind me.

There's literally nowhere to put it. "On top of the stove, I guess."

"How's everyone doing out there?"

Laughter, and easy conversation comes from the other room. "It sounds like it's going great. I think Tiffany and Audrey are feeling Angie out. Making sure she'll be a suitable friend for me."

"The three of you are so freaking weird."

I shrug my shoulders, "Would you have me any other way?"

"Oh, I can think of a few ways I'd like to have you," he wraps his arms around me.

I grab a spoon out of the drawer and smack him with it before adding it to one of the dishes Angie brought. It's nice having all of my things here with me. I've really made the space my own. I'll stay here as long as I can afford it. I put most of my bonus from Mr. Hart in savings. It's a nice cushion for when things are slow at Out of the Ashes. Angie has been amazing to work with, and she likes having the breaks she gets since I've come on as assistant manager. All of the social media marketing I've put in place has helped bring more people into the bar. She's flourishing and I love being a part of that.

"Is the food ready, yet?" Tiffany stomps into the kitchen. "I'm wasting away over here."

"I swear you care more about food than you do anything else."

"I do when I haven't eaten all day," she pouts.

"You better watch it," Johnny steps away from me. "You put her in charge of finding you a roommate. She'll pick someone horrible if you aren't nice to her."

"I'm more worried about whatever food she cooked," Tiffany ducks out of the way of the towel I throw at her head. "What? It's true. Your cooking is shit."

"Don't worry, I didn't make anything." I step around the counter and walk into the living. "Everything is ready."

Our friends start filing into the kitchen. Reaf, his wife and their daughter at the front of the line. Tiffany is right behind them with Audrey and Angie bringing up the back.

Seeing all of our friends in one place warms my heart. I've grown so much since moving here, and feel lucky to have relationships outside of my bond with my cousins. They'll always be my best friends, but it's nice having other people I can talk to. Ones that are a hell of a lot closer than four hours away.

Once everyone has their plates filled to the brim, they take a seat at the table. Johnny and I are last. Being a hostess is a completely new thing to me, and I'll have to do it again when we get together with our families for Thanksgiving. Hopefully none of them are expecting me to cook anything. I'll find the nearest place that caters to avoid embarrassing myself.

"I'd like to make a toast," Johnny announces to the room. Everyone pauses in their eating, except for Layla, Reaf's cutie of a daughter. She's eating with gusto. "Thank you all for being here tonight. We hope to have more get togethers, like this in the future. Stella, you literally crashed into my life, and have made it better every single day." I blush at his words. "Thank you for not killing me when I messed up your car worse than it was. You truly are the best thing in my life."

"Ditto," I agree.

"And because I know you won't cuss me out in front of a room full of people, or a toddler, I want to ask you a question." Oh shit, he's not about to propose is he. I can't handle that shit right now. It's way too soon for that. "Will you move in with me?"

I breathe a sigh of relief. That I can handle. "That depends. Is that stupid hole in the floor fixed?" That earns some chuckles from our guests.

"It will be if you say yes."

"Will you promise to keep all creepy crawly things out of the house? Oh, and not to turn into a serial killer?" That last question didn't earn as many laughs as the first two.

"Yes. I'll do my best to keep snakes out of the bathroom." He looks around the room. "As for becoming a serial killer…I have no plans on that happening. I'll let you know if it changes, though."

"Then yes. I'll move in with you." He pulls me into his arms, and slams his mouth into mine. Everyone hoots and hollers, celebrating with us. Even Layla can be heard over everyone else.

"You've just made me the happiest man in the room."

"Good. I'll make you even happier later." I whisper in his ear. "Let's hang out with our friends before we run them out of the house."

"I'm not opposed to that."

"Shut up and eat."

Tiffany claps her hands together, silencing everyone. "That's enough PDA for the evening. I'm going to lose my appetite."

"Fine," I laugh. "Let's eat."

Life can't get more perfect than it is right now.

Did you enjoy Gone Country? Grab Tiffany's story in Gone Steady, and turn the page for a peek at the first chapter.

Want deleted scenes from Gone Country? Sign up for my newsletter to get a free ebook with scenes from Johnny's perspective.

You can also grab a copy of Johnny and Stella's wedding story by signing up for my newsletter!

Chapter 1

The bass is thrumming through my body. Bodies pressed against each other as the music flows through the crowd. This is my happy place. Audrey and Stella being here is the only thing that would make tonight even better. But no, Stella had to go off and get into a committed relationship. Don't get me wrong, I'm happy for her and she deserves all the happiness in the world. It's just that she's four hours away and can't join me on my adventures anymore.

Audrey on the other hand is lame. This isn't her scene, so I don't blame her completely. I just need them here to keep my crazy ass in line. Hopefully they're busy finding a roommate for me that I get along with. The last few they've picked have been complete duds. They need to stop thinking about what their likes and dislikes are, and start thinking about how I feel about them. Too bad I can't be trusted to pick my own damn roommate. My bullshit radar is on the fritz and the last few people I've moved into my apartment have been horrible choices.

The band on stage begins playing a cover of "The

Chapter 1

Imperial March," and as much as I don't care for Star Wars, I can't deny that the rock edge they put on it is amazing. It's enough to have me jumping up and down and acting like a damn fool. This is what I live for. Getting lost in the music and giving up any worry I have over finding the perfect roommate or living up to the same expectations as my cousins. If my mom, or dad, mention how proud they are of my cousins one more time, I'm going to lose my shit.

The band switches to a cover of Nirvana, and I sing at the top of my lungs. Putting all my frustration at being the family screwup into every single word. Being serious is overrated. I love my life. I only need to live up to my own expectations and flutter wherever the wind takes me. It may have caused me to make a few bad decisions along the way, but I don't regret any of them. Who needs a steady nine to five job? Not me. I won't be happy in that type of environment. And if I did have that job, my ass wouldn't be at a concert on a weeknight, having an incredible time.

Someone bumps into me from behind, breaking my doom and gloom thoughts, and I fall to the ground.

A man looms over me, his lips moving, but I can't hear what he's saying.

"What?" I scream to be heard above the roaring crowd.

He bends closer, his eyes hidden behind square black frames, brows furrowed. "Are you hurt?" He holds his hand out to help me up. It takes me by surprise.

"I-I don't think so," I reach for his hand and allow him to pull me up. "You kind of came out of nowhere."

"I'm so sorry," he brings me closer to him so he doesn't have to yell. "I didn't mean to plow you over. The assholes back there are being kinda pushy."

Chapter 1

Most girls would flinch at being so close to someone they don't know. Not me. All I want to do is get to know him a little better. "It's okay." He opens his mouth to protest, but I cut him off. "We are in the pit." I stare at him for emphasis. "The likelihood of me getting jostled around is pretty high."

"Jostled and getting your ass knocked to the ground are two very different things." His dark brown eyes study me. What is he looking for?

"Seriously, I'm good." I turn back toward the stage, ready to rock out. This guy is cute and all but he can't give me the high music gives me. Not yet, anyway. After a few more drinks that may change.

Tap. Tap. Tap. A finger raps on my shoulder. "Are you sure?" I'm not even fully facing him before the words are out of his mouth.

Do I blow him off? That is the big question of the night. He's not too shabby to look at. And he's kind. A little too kind. "If you really want to make it up to me, you can buy me a drink." I'm not above getting free drinks.

"I can definitely do that." He begins walking toward the bar area, and stops. "Want to come with me?"

Not really. I love this band, and I don't want to miss any part of their set. On the other hand, he's kind of cute, and he did help me up after knocking me over. The fact that I've seen this band almost ten times is what prompts me to hook my arm into his. "Sure."

We push our way through the crowd, trying to keep from getting jostled around. It shouldn't be this hard to get out of the pit. It never has been before. The fans are amped up, though. It'll be almost impossible for us to get back in the area we just left.

"What's your name?" My new, bespectacled friend

Chapter 1

asks. His mouth is near my ear to be heard over the crowd, and a shiver runs down my spine. I'd be lying if I said that's never happened before. I'm no stranger to lust, and this guy fits the bill.

"Tiffany," I yell, unsure if he can hear me over the roar of the crowd.

Finally, we get to the exit. Once we leave the main concert area, the noise dies down and everything feels muted. It's crazy how one thick wall can change the sound of everything, even in an open air venue. "What's your name?" My voice is louder than necessary, still adjusting to the quieter atmosphere.

He chuckles and removes his arm from mine. Nobody has ever done that before, and the rejection stings. "It's Spencer."

"Do you live in Austin?"

"Yeah," he leads us toward the closest vendor. "I've lived here all my life." The woman behind the counter asks for our ID's. "What do you want to drink?"

"I'm not picky, you choose." Neither one of my cousins would be able to do that. They typically drink the same thing no matter where they go. Stella is the only one broadening her horizons since she started working at that bar in Asheville. She's acting like all of these drinks are new just because she's never had them before.

"You're pretty brave," he grins. "I could be picking out something horrible for you to drink and you wouldn't even know it."

I shrug my shoulders and lean against the sticky counter. "I guess it's a good thing I know what most of these beers taste like."

"Very clever," he taps me on the nose and orders our drinks. "Back to our earlier conversation." Shit, what were

Chapter 1

we talking about. "Do you live in the area?" Oh, right. We were talking about living in Austin.

The band starts a new song and a part of me is itching to go back to the pit, but this guy is nice. It wouldn't be a horrible decision to see where tonight may lead. I'm not getting any bad vibes off of him, so all is good. "Yep. I've lived here for a few years."

"What made you pick Austin?"

"My cousins." It's as simple as that. Stella was already here, but when Audrey moved… I didn't want to be stuck in our small town by myself. Moving to a big city seemed like a good thing to do, and the adventures I could have here were endless.

"Most people try to get away from their families, not run to them," he laughs.

"They're my best friends. Being around them and seeing them all the time is fun." Until they get all judge-y and get on my nerves. Even then, I love them and can't imagine being away from them. "Now, it's kind of boring since my oldest cousin moved away. Audrey doesn't like to go to these things unless Stella is with us."

"That's a shame." He shakes his head and looks toward the crowd we were just in. "If you ever need someone to join you for live music, I'm available."

Whoah. Wait a hot damn minute. Is he trying to ask me on possible future dates, or is he just making small talk to make me feeling better? I'm not that type of girl. I don't do multiple dates, at least not for long. That one statement shouldn't shake me up this much. My good sense is being distracted by his looks and how easy he is to talk to.

"We'll see." I shrug, hoping the answer is as noncommittal as possible. I wouldn't be opposed to seeing him again, but I plan for concerts months in advance. Hell, I

Chapter 1

had tickets for my cousins for this one, but Audrey bailed last minute, and Stella was busy with her new job in Asheville.

We grab our beers and instead of returning to the pit, we find an open spot on the lawn. It's easier to talk up here while enjoying the music. "So, what do you do for a living?"

"I'm a waitress at a restaurant downtown." I wait for the look of horror to cross his face, or for him to decide that I don't have any aspirations. You'd be surprised how many times I'm asked when I'm going to get a real job. For me, this is a real job. I enjoy what I do, and I don't think I should make apologies for it.

To my surprise he doesn't say one bad thing. "How do you not get tired standing in the pit after you've been on your feet all day?"

"It's an entirely different kind of energy when I'm at a concert."

"That makes sense," he nods. We watch the remainder of the show in silence, soaking up the music and enjoying the night air. Once the band finishes their encore song, we stay seated while everyone gets up in droves to walk to their cars. "Did you drive here?"

"No, I took an Uber. I don't like driving if there's a chance I'll be drinking." I grab my phone to let Audrey know the show is over. She may not be here, but I at least like to let her know I'm safe.

"Any chance you want to grab something to eat with me?" His eyes are on the ground while he asks, unsure of what I'll say.

"Sure," I say. "How do pancakes sound?"

We get up and walk to the exit of the venue. "I'll get us a ride."

Chapter 1

"Thanks." Phone still in hand, I send a group text to Audrey and Stella.

Tiffany: Concert is done. Having dinner with a fellow concert goer.
Stella: Is he hot?
Tiffany: Who said it was a "he"?
Audrey: Because when isn't it a he?
Tiffany: You have a point.
Audrey: Turn on your location sharing so I know you're safe.
Tiffany: Yes, Mom."
Stella: Have fun. Don't do anything I wouldn't do.
Tiffany: Do you know who you're talking to? Besides, it's not like I'll ever see him again.
Audrey: I'm not kidding. TURN IT ON!
Stella: You better do it. Call me tomorrow with all the details. Also, I think I found the perfect roommate for you.
Tiffany: You got it.

I turn on the location sharing on my phone. If I don't Audrey will bug the hell out of me until I do. I can't have her cramping my style tonight. I have every intention of going home with this guy. The Uber he requested pulls up to the curb. "After you," he opens the door and I slide into the backseat.

He sits beside me instead of the front seat, and I know he's definitely interested. "Want to get those pancakes to go?"

Acknowledgments

This book was a long time coming, and took on many variations. I honestly couldn't have gotten through writing this book with my best friends. Nessa, Kelsie, Tasha, and Cindy, y'all pushed me to finish this book, and I'm beyond grateful for y'all.

My Alphas... you ladies rock. You have no idea how much your help means to me.

Victoria and Shelly, thank you for polishing this beauty up. Your insight means so much to me. A Novel Idea Services... You put together a beautiful cover, and nailed it when I didn't know what I wanted.

Mom and Dad, just thank you for everything.

Hubs, Boy Child & Wee One, I love y'all to the moon and back.

Dreamers, thank you for helping me name some of the people and places in this book. Y'all are amazing!!!

Readers, thank you for reading this. You're the reason I do what I do.

Also by Katrina Marie

Cousins Gone RomCom Series

Gone Country

Gone Steady

Gone Inn

Gone Before

Gone Again

Out of the Ashes Series

The Taking Chances Series

Cocky Hero Club

Big Baller

Baseball & Broadway